## "Luke!"
## she called

The name was half choked as it left her lips. He didn't turn around.

She hastened her step. He had reached the table where they had sat four years before. He paused at the same chair he had occupied. She was certain now, and she ran the last couple of yards.

"Luke!" But all her wild elation burst as the man turned toward her. The face was one she'd never seen before. A black patch covered one eye, and a prominent scar sliced through the eyebrow above the patch.

But Genevra didn't care. Shock gave way to a surge of fierce love. She waited for him to nod, to say yes, to acknowledge his identity... waited in growing desperation.

"I'm afraid you're mistaken." His voice was soft, but the accent was unmistakably American... not Australian!

"My name is Nemo," he continued steadily. "Christian Nemo."

**EMMA DARCY** nearly became an actress until her fiancé declared he preferred to attend the theatre *with* her. She became a wife and mother. Later she took up oil painting—unsuccessfully, she remarks. Then, she tried architecture, designing the family home in New South Wales. Next came romance writing—"the hardest and most challenging of all the activities," she confesses.

## Books by Emma Darcy

# EMMA DARCY

## always love

**Harlequin Books**

TORONTO • NEW YORK • LONDON
AMSTERDAM • PARIS • SYDNEY • HAMBURG
STOCKHOLM • ATHENS • TOKYO • MILAN

Harlequin Presents first edition March 1989
ISBN 0-373-11151-7

Original hardcover edition published in 1988
by Mills & Boon Limited

# CHAPTER ONE

GENEVRA could not eat the lunch she had ordered. The tension inside her grew with every passing minute that brought her closer and closer to the meeting with Matthew. Finally she left the hotel dining-room and returned to her room, where she paced the floor, trying to calm her inner agitation.

She had made the right decision, no question about it. Her mind was made up, and she was not going to be diverted from her purpose, regardless of what Matthew said. She had to find out about Luke, and Matthew was the only one who could help her. He wouldn't approve of the course she had set her mind on, but that didn't matter. Only learning the truth about Luke mattered. She could no longer bear not knowing.

Luke had loved her. The bond between them had been too strong for Genevra to ever doubt that. They had spent six weeks together...six weeks of long, magical days that she would never forget...a romantic dream that had come true.

He had come into her bookshop at St Ives one bright spring morning; a tall, darkly tanned, and very handsome stranger...an Australian, she quickly discovered, in England on business. But he was taking a holiday break and he found the fishing village of St Ives fascinating. More fascinating by the minute!

Their eyes had sparkled at each other, and Luke had stayed in the shop, chatting to her in between customers. The holiday break had been extended, and extended again, until the call came from home, pleading for his immediate return. His sister was very ill, asking for him. Luke had left within twenty-four hours, and Genevra had never seen him again. The letter had come a month later.

The shock and the pain of it still lingered in her heart, and she had read the words so many times, they were indelibly printed in her memory.

'My darling Genevra,

I don't know how to write what I must. I know too well the pain it will give you, and wish with all my heart that I did not have to make this choice, but I cannot turn my back on the love and obligations I owe my family. I could not be happy within myself, nor could I make you happy, knowing I had refused to answer their needs when they have given me so much.

I cannot marry you as we planned, Genevra, and I will not ask you to wait for me. I must honour the commitment I am about to make for as long as it lasts. By the time you receive this letter, I will be married.

It will be best for both of us to try and forget
what could have been. Goodbye, my love.'

'Goodbye...', 'forget what could have been...'
But Genevra had not been able to forget the love
they had shared, nor bring herself to really believe
in his goodbye. The hurt had been unbearable. To
lose the man she loved to another woman, when
she had only just learnt she was carrying his
child... Genevra had been unable to accept it. She
had read and re-read behind the lines of that letter.

Luke had been forced into a marriage he didn't
want, to a woman he didn't love, and whatever the
pressures that had driven him into such a course
they would lessen in time. If she waited long
enough, he would come back to her. He would free
himself of that woman as soon as he could do so
without hurting his family, and then...

But he hadn't come back, nor had there been one
word from him in all that time, and Genevra
couldn't bear to go on waiting any longer. Time
had eroded her certainty in his love for her. If Luke
was still married, then it was because he wanted to
be, and she had been deluding herself with a dream
that would never come true. It was better to know
than to go on dreaming... wasn't it?

She suddenly caught her reflection in the mirror
and paused in mid-step. If Luke walked back into
her life today, would he still think her beautiful?
The years had changed her. The experience of being

a single parent had slimmed her girlish face into the firmer lines of a woman, and the curves of her figure had become more pronounced. Motherhood had dropped her waistline and brought a larger fullness to her breasts, as well as sharpening her mind to the harsher realities of life.

She had kept her black hair long because Luke had liked it that way, its thick waves rippling from a centre parting to cloud around her pale, oval face and long, slender neck. But the warm innocence had long since disappeared from her eyes, and the mental and emotional torment of the last few days had taken its toll. The thickly fringed blue eyes were startlingly dark—glittering bruises in a face that seemed too delicate to support them. Her straight, little nose had a pinched look about the nostrils, and her normally soft, generous mouth was a tight red line.

The navy-blue suit and the white silk shirt emphasised her pallor, a mistake that was too late to correct. But that didn't matter, either. She wasn't going to see Luke. She hadn't seen him for four years, and today... today was the day of decision. All she had to do was confront Matthew and tell him what she wanted, and then, with her mind free of this turmoil, she could meet the American publisher, Christian Nemo, with more equanimity than she could manage now.

It was the American's letter that had started this present torment over Luke, sharpening the ache in her heart. If Christian Nemo hadn't asked her to meet him at the Dorchester Hotel for afternoon tea, reminding her of that last afternoon with Luke... but it was time she did something positive, instead of blindly waiting for a man who might never return to her.

She almost jumped when the telephone rang, and her hand was trembling as she picked up the receiver.

'Miss Kingsley?'

'Yes.'

'Reception desk. Mr Hastings' car is here for you, Miss Kingsley.'

'Thank you.'

She glanced anxiously at her watch as she snatched up her handbag. It was only one-twenty; Matthew was ten minutes early. She had meant to be in the foyer, waiting for him. As it was, he had done her the favour of fitting her into his busy schedule at late notice.

Her heart fluttered with nervous apprehension as she hurried downstairs and out to the white Rolls-Royce which stood at the kerb. The chauffeur had the passenger door open for her, and she quickly slid in next to Matthew.

She flicked him an apologetic look. 'I didn't expect you this soon.'

As usual, he looked very much the eminent solicitor. The shock of white hair gave him the distinguished air of a patriarch. His face had the weathered strength of character that shouted of an ingrained discipline of mind. He wore respectability like a well-fitted glove, his dark suit the epitome of conventional quality, his manner impeccably that of a gentleman, born and bred. He projected the image one expected of a top solicitor from Gray's Inn.

He shook his head at her in fond indulgence. 'Genevra, why do you persist in staying at a hotel in Bloomsbury when you come up to London? There is no need...'

'It suits me,' Genevra cut in quickly, tired of Matthew's attempts to get her to spend the trust money that he administered for her.

He sighed. 'You can afford better, Genevra. It's absolutely ridiculous that...'

She turned on him, too wrought up to be patient. 'I've told you, Matthew. I'm saving that money for Johnny. It's his birthright. I'll spend it if I need to, but I'm doing quite well without it. I can make a reasonable living out of the bookshop, and I'm even seeing a publisher later today about a book he wants to commission.'

'That's splendid!' he said, obviously pleased for her. 'But even so, those two tourist books you wrote have only brought in a few hundred pounds, and the bookshop provides little more than subsistence living. The point is, my dear, that *you* are the beneficiary of the Anna Christie Trust, not your son.'

But she wasn't really. Genevra had never felt right about that money, even though Matthew had assured her from the very beginning that it was legally hers, to do with as she wished. She had needed it then. Needed it desperately. Luke had gone, she was carrying their child, and her father had left a mountain of debts on the bookshop which was her only means of support. It wasn't until after all the debts had been paid and she had given birth to Johnny that Genevra began to wonder...and it had preyed on her mind all these years, just as Luke had. So why not find out about that, too?

'Matthew, that's one of the things I would like you to do for me.'

The words burst off her tongue with more force than she had intended, and Matthew raised his eyebrows in surprised enquiry.

'I want you to find out about Anna Christie,' she said, in a more subdued voice, but with no less conviction.

He gave one of his dismissive shrugs. 'There's nothing to find out. I've told you all I know. She was a Canadian.'

'Haven't you ever thought it strange?' Genevra persisted, wanting his understanding. 'You know what my circumstances were at the time—three

months pregnant with Johnny, threatened with
bankruptcy, no one to turn to for help. Maybe I
would have survived anyway, but it was the lowest
point of my life. And suddenly...there was the
Anna Christie Trust!'

'God looks after his angels!' His hands gesticu-
lated the dismissal of any fanciful nonsense as he
addressed himself to her more seriously. 'What do
you want to believe? That a woman on the other
side of the Atlantic Ocean died for your con-
venience? You weren't even named in the trust deed,
Genevra. It was your father who was the beneficiary, and then his next of kin. If you had not survived your father, the money would have gone to
the International Red Cross.'

'Why should some woman I've never heard of
leave all that money to my father? It doesn't make
sense!' Genevra retorted in bewilderment.

Matthew sighed and linked his hands across his
pin-striped waistcoat. It was a mannerism that indicated he was about to give her the wisdom of his
sixty years. At another time, Genevra would have
smiled and accepted that he knew better than she
did, but not today.

'Maybe she once loved your father. Maybe he
saved her life. Who knows? Obviously there was
some connection between them, probably before
you were ever born. It doesn't matter.'

'It matters to me,' she said stubbornly. 'I want to know, Matthew. I've lived too long with the torment of wondering about things. From this day onwards, I'm going to learn what I want to know.'

He stared at her, frowning over the glittering determination in her eyes. His hands slowly lifted in a gesture of submission. 'So be it, then. I'll contact the Canadian firm of solicitors who set up the trust for Anna Christie. If they can't come up with the information you want, then we can proceed with an investigation.'

'Thank you.' She knew Matthew was indulging her, and she felt a rush of affection for the kindly old solicitor for conceding to her point of view without too much argument. She hoped he would not feel it necessary to caution her against her next request, because it was the really important one.

The Rolls-Royce pulled up outside Matthew's chambers at Gray's Inn. Genevra tried to get her thoughts in some coherent order as Matthew led her inside. She had to say what she had come to say, but the pain inside her was like the growth of a terminal illness that was about to be openly confronted.

Matthew closed the door of his office behind them, escorted Genevra to a chair, then rounded the huge mahogany desk and dropped into the leather chair behind it.

The Anna Christie file was already on the desk in front of him. It was the only business that ever brought Genevra to these chambers, and undoubtedly Matthew's secretary had placed it there. Matthew opened it, made a note, then closed it again, looking up at her with an encouraging smile.

'Sit down, Genevra. You can tell me now what the real problem is.'

But she couldn't sit down. Her nerves were jumping too much. For a moment, she panicked. Did she really want to know? Yes, came the agonised cry from her heart. But, despite her resolution, despite the need churning through her, Genevra could not hold Matthew's enquiring gaze. She fumbled open her handbag, withdrew the card on which she had written Luke's name and the only address he had given her, and placed it on Matthew's desk.

A self-conscious flush burnt a swift path up her throat and into her cheeks, and she turned away, pacing distractedly around the room as she forced the words out, all too painfully aware of the strained stiffness of her voice.

'There's a man I want to find out about. His name is Stanford...Luke Stanford. He's an Australian, an engineer...thirty-three years old. The last I heard of him, he was living in New South Wales. Near Sydney. But the address I've written on that card is four years old. He may not be there any more. He...he married at about that time.'

Tears pricked her eyes and she fought them back. She had made up her mind. She couldn't go on waiting, not knowing what had happened, not knowing if he ever really meant to come back to her. She blinked hard and fought down the lump in her throat. Then, with unflinching determination, she swung around and defiantly met the eyes of the man whose help was absolutely critical to her cause.

'I want to find out if he's still married. Can you arrange that for me, Matthew?'

His whole face seemed to sag with a sad weariness as he looked down at his hands. For long, tense moments his fingers dragged at the age-spots on the skin just above the knuckles. 'I take it that Luke Stanford is Johnny's father.'

It was not a question. It was a flat statement of fact, carefully drained of any emotion. He lifted his eyes and the knowledge in them was tempered by a sympathy that recognised and understood human failings all too well.

'Yes.' She almost choked on the word. She had never told anyone outside her family before, but it was the obvious answer, and there was no point in denying it. Yet it was not for Johnny's sake that she had to find out about Luke. Her three-year-old son wasn't eating his heart out for a father he had never known. It was for herself. Even after four years of silence, she could not stop loving Luke Stanford.

Matthew nodded. His gaze slowly swept back to her, and his mouth took on a sad, ironic twist as he spoke. 'I know you don't want to hear the advice I'm about to give, Genevra, but I would not be serving you well if I don't give it.'

He paused to lend emphasis to his words. 'Let the past go. You're only twenty-five, young enough and beautiful enough to attract any number of men. Don't look back, Genevra. Look forward. And open your heart to what can be...for your sake, and Johnny's sake.'

She shook her head. He didn't understand. Even if she showed him Luke's letter, he wouldn't understand. He hadn't known Luke as she had known him. 'I can't do that, Matthew. Maybe...after I know...I can do what you say. But not until then.'

Matthew's face hardened. 'Genevra, he left you to marry another woman. He left you carrying his child...'

'Luke didn't know that!' she cried, her eyes painfully protesting against the accusation. 'And I don't intend to tell him. I have no intention of interfering with...with his life, Matthew. I don't want him to know anything about this inquiry. I just want to know if he's still married. I need to know. That's all,' she pleaded.

'It will only bring you grief.'

'No more than I've lived with for the past four years. Grief is nothing new to me, Matthew.'

The passionate conviction of her retort won a reprieve from argument. Matthew's mouth tightened over whatever he had been about to say. His gaze dropped to the card she had placed on his desk. He picked it up, fingering it with an air of distaste. Disapproval emanated from him but, when he finally spoke, it was with curt decisiveness.

'I don't personally know of any private investigation firms in Australia, but I have contacts who can advise me. I'll let you know as soon as I get the information you want; and I'll insist that all inquiries be carried out with maximum discretion.'

Genevra almost sagged with relief. Her legs started to shake. She put out a hand and gripped the back of a chair to steady herself. 'Thank you,' she whispered, her voice deserting her now that the battle had been won.

Matthew's gaze shot up to pin hers. 'I hope this will be the finish of it, Genevra.'

No, it would never be finished, Genevra thought with a dull sense of resignation, but she didn't say that. 'At least then I'll know,' she replied on a wistful sigh.

And that was all she could achieve, hopeless as that might prove to be. But the wheels had been set in motion. The waiting and wondering would soon be over. And then...then she would know if her life was ever again to have any meaning.

# CHAPTER TWO

MATTHEW insisted that Genevra take his car to her appointment with Christian Nemo. He had always been kind to her and, despite their sharp difference of opinion, he seemed even more solicitous than usual as he escorted her out of his chambers; asking after Johnny and Auntie May and their life in St Ives, handing her into the Rolls-Royce himself, and wishing her all the best with the publisher.

Genevra thanked him once again, but she was relieved when he finally shut the car door, releasing her from the strain of his presence. The memory of their altercation over Luke was still pulsing painfully.

She asked the chauffeur to drop her off at one of the entrances to Hyde Park. Although her talk with Matthew had seemed to go on for an eternity, she still had more than half an hour to fill in before she had to be at the Dorchester.

She relaxed back into the plush leather seat of the Rolls and closed her eyes, half regretting what she had just done.

She felt curiously drained, almost as if she had betrayed a trust she should have kept. But the silence had been too long. Even the most desperate hope needed something to feed on.

'Hyde Park, madam.'

Genevra jolted upright. The car was stationary, and the chauffeur had opened the door for her. She stepped out on to the pavement, thanked the man, and walked briskly into the park.

It was a fine, sunny day, the trees a vibrant summer green, roses coming into bloom, the rolling expanse of grass invitingly lush. Just as it had been that last day with Luke.

The sweet memories crept into her mind: lounging on the grass under the trees, idly watching others play makeshift games of soccer and baseball while she and Luke talked...and touched; strolling around the Serpentine, feeding the swans, laughing at the amateur canoeists...loving one another.

As she walked along, Genevra felt a strong sense of all that had happened before; past and present in parallel time-streams...shifting, crossing, merging into one. Luke's presence was so strong that she could almost imagine he was walking beside her, as he had done on that last afternoon, four years ago, taking her to afternoon tea at the Dorchester Hotel.

Genevra had never indulged in such luxury before or since, but Luke had wanted to take her somewhere special. It was something of a tradition in

London, afternoon tea at the Dorchester, but not for ordinary people like her, of course.

The snobbery of England meant nothing to Luke. She had wanted a cup of tea, and he had insisted on taking her to the most prestigious place in London. He had blithely swept aside all her protests that they were not dressed correctly and they couldn't really go *there*!

She remembered how awed she had felt as they waited at the entrance to the Promenade Room until a waiter in black tails and white bow-tie had come to show them to a table. The room glowed so richly, with its long colonnade of marble columns veined in a soft russet and topped with bands of beautifully worked gilt. The ceiling was indented with gilt friezes, and huge cages made of glass and brass hung from it, glittering with the candles that lit the room. Other candle-fittings were centred on wall mirrors, and between the mirrors were quiet paintings, lending further elegance to the unique ambience of the room.

Between the columns were beautiful potted palms, surrounded by trailing vines, and Indian statues from the British Raj. A grand piano of polished red mahogany sat in the centre of the room, and an accomplished pianist played a selection of songs from popular musicals.

Genevra had clung nervously to Luke's arm as the waiter led them down the room, past the groupings of sofas and chairs that were so richly upholstered in red and gold striped velvet. Softly patterned carpets in tonings of red and green and peach were set into the grey and white marble slabs on the floor. Genevra had watched her footing, terrified that she might trip and make a fool of herself.

Not only was the room the last word in elegant luxury, the tea service was exquisite: starched white linen serviettes, silver teapots, sugar bowls, tea strainers, milk and cream jugs; delicate china crockery; dainty little pots of jam, rosettes of butter, scones, cakes, a selection of finger sandwiches served from a silver tray with silver tongs.

And the patrons had been equally fascinating: groups of stylish Americans, the British upper class with their careless arrogance, the beautifully mannered Orientals...Genevra had stared unashamedly at an Arab sheik who had walked by.

Luke, in his egalitarian Australian way, had laughed her out of her sense of awe, taking all the fabulous service for granted since he was paying for it, and making up wicked stories about the people around them. He had made it a magical experience, one she would remember vividly all her life...even if he never came back to her.

Genevra paused on the footpath just across from the Dorchester, waiting for a break in the traffic. She watched the hotel doorman, in his top hat and tails, opening the passenger door of a Silver Cloud

Rolls-Royce. An ironic smile curled her mouth.
After four years of friendly association with
Matthew Hastings, she was no longer in awe of
luxury cars or places.

All the same, the Dorchester Hotel seemed an
odd choice of venue for a meeting with a publisher.
But Mr Christian Nemo was an American. While
in London, he probably enjoyed tasting the best of
English traditional fare.

The traffic break came, and she quickly crossed
the road. It was just three o'clock as she walked
into the hotel foyer.

Her eye was immediately caught by the magnificent hydrangeas in the two huge urns which stood
like sentinels on either side of the entrance to the
Promenade Room. She paused there, admiring the
huge blooms, until a girl in a smart black suit en-
quired if she could be of service.

'Yes. I'm to meet a Mr Christian Nemo,' Genevra
explained, flicking a look down the length of the
room to see if she could spot a lone gentleman. 'I
believe he has...'

Shock cut off her speech. The man walking past
the piano to the far end of the room... she could
not believe her eyes! Even from the back view, she
couldn't be mistaken. His height, the shape of his
head, the close-set ears, the bulk of his shoulders,
the way his thick, dark hair curled around the nape
of his neck. It had to be him!

For a moment she was totally mesmerised, unable to move or even breathe. Then her heart started to pound, sending painful vibrations through her chest. A great welling of love poured through her body. No matter that her mind told her it was impossible. She could not doubt the truth of what she saw.

Genevra didn't stop to think, to reconsider. Her heart was pounding faster than a jackhammer now. She brushed past the girl and barely restrained herself from breaking into a run. 'Luke!' she called, the name half choked as it left her lips. He didn't turn around.

She hastened her step. He had reached the table where they had sat four years before. He paused at the same chair he had occupied. She was certain now. Excitement pumped her heart even faster. She did run the last couple of yards and grabbed his arm before he could sit down.

'Luke!' she breathed ecstatically, but all her wild elation burst into a thousand stabbing icicles as the man turned slowly towards her.

The face was one she had never seen before, cruelly hurt in some accident a long time ago. A black patch covered one eye, and the skin of his face was marked with a faint criss-crossing of pale lines, the result of an immense amount of corrective surgery. A more prominent scar sliced through the eyebrow above the patch. The jawline was subtly different to Luke's, not so square; and the shape of the nose...it wasn't right, either.

But Genevra did not care. Shock gave way to a surge of fierce love. If it was Luke, she would throw herself into his arms and kiss away the pain of all those terrible injuries. She waited for him to nod, to say yes, to acknowledge his identity...waited in growing desperation for a sign that never came.

'I'm afraid you are mistaken, young lady.'

His voice was soft, kindly, but the accent was unmistakably American...not Australian! His gaze held hers steadily, without flinching.

'My name is Nemo,' he continued slowly. 'Christian Nemo.'

## CHAPTER THREE

'No!'

The word exploded from Genevra before she could control herself. Shock had shattered into violent disbelief. She half raised her hand in negation of what he had said, and barely stopped herself from accusing him of playing some cruel trick on her.

She had been so sure, so certain that the man was Luke, that he had come back for her. Until she saw his face, heard his accent, she would have sworn on a stack of Bibles that this man standing in front of her had to be Luke.

Yet how could she deny the evidence of her eyes and ears? The face...the voice...both of them contradicted her conviction so strongly. In sheer desperation, she searched for something that would confirm the identity of the man beyond question.

Luke's eyes had been gray.

Christian Nemo's were a tawny brown.

The blood drained from Genevra's head. A trembling weakness seeped into her legs. She swayed on her feet as the realisation of how wrong she had been hit home.

The man clutched her arm hard, steadying her. 'I'm sorry. I know my face comes as a bit of a shock to most people.' His mouth curled into a twist of self-mockery. 'That's why I chose the most unobtrusive table in this room. I don't wish to put people off their afternoon tea.'

'It's not that bad,' Genevra blurted out, instinctively protesting his misreading of her reaction, even as she struggled to accept that he wasn't Luke. This was the man she had come to meet, the American publisher whom she had wanted to impress!

The blood came rushing back to her face in a heated burst of embarrassment. 'What I mean is...' She floundered, searching for some tactful way to explain her mistake. 'I thought you were someone else, you see. It was so stupid of me. You must think I'm quite mad.'

'No. Our minds play all sorts of tricks on us at times. I'm sorry I've upset you, however unwittingly it was. Would you like to sit down for a few moments?'

His kindness made Genevra feel worse. Any chance of carrying off this introduction with dignity was long gone. All she could do now was give him the courtesy of looking him straight in the eye while she owned up to her own identity.

'The fact is, Mr Nemo, I'm Genevra Kingsley, and I hope you can overlook my...'

'Miss Kingsley!' Warm pleasure lighted his expression and softened the harsh lines of his face, making him look more open and approachable. He released his grasp on her arm and took her hand in his. 'I am delighted to meet you. I must confess I was expecting someone not . . . quite so beautiful.'

The smile, the way his fingers had curled around hers, the tingling reaction to the light pressure of his hand . . . God! She was going mad! If he wasn't Luke . . . But he had denied that he was, and she had to make some reply.

'That's very kind of you.'

She was so frozen and confused inside, she wondered how she got the words out.

'Do please sit down,' he invited.

Genevra sat, concentrating hard on pulling herself together. Luke had been so heavily on her mind that she had obviously projected her need for him on to this man. That he had looked exactly like Luke from a back view was simply an uncanny coincidence. She was lucky that Christian Nemo was generous enough to forgive her blunder.

She watched him lower himself into a chair, noticing for the first time that he used a walking cane—black oak, with a silver tip and a chased silver knob. His left leg obviously gave him some trouble, although he had not walked with any stiffness. She couldn't quite fit that elegant walking-cane with her image of Luke, nor the conservative cut of the dark grey suit. The quality tailoring, the silk stripe in his white shirt, the rich statement of the red and silver tie—they added up to a man who put considerable stock in his appearance...or a man who wanted to create that impression.

The clothes did not disguise the toughness of his physique: the broad chest and muscular shoulders, the strength in his hands. In some strange way, his facial disfigurement actually enhanced the aura of masculinity, suggesting that he would always rise above any adversity, unbeaten.

His lips curved into a dry smile under her intense scrutiny. 'Beauty and the Beast?' he drawled, making light of her rudeness in staring.

'No!' Genevra retorted sharply, distressed by a reference which was so demeaning to himself. She imagined the mountain of hurts that had forced the building of such a flippant façade, and her stomach churned with hatred for all the people who had made him feel so conscious of his scars. If he had been Luke... Without giving it another second's thought, Genevra burst into speech, defending him from himself as well as other people.

'If you want me to stay, I don't want to hear you talk like that! Never again! I can't tolerate your thinking of yourself in...in such terms. I won't stand for it!'

Her chest was heaving with the expulsion of her pent-up emotion and, as the last word of her ultimatum faded into a dreadful silence, Genevra wished the floor would open up and swallow her. Christian Nemo wouldn't want to do business with her after that outburst. Yet she had only spoken the truth. She couldn't have borne to have him talk about himself in such a way.

His face had stiffened in mute shock. They stared at each other like grim antagonists. Genevra felt drained, but the tension emanating from him kept her nerves on edge. It was a relief when he finally broke the silence.

'You speak just as you write, Miss Kingsley. Directly, and without pretension.'

His stiff manner of speech contrasted sharply to the pleasant flow of his previous statements, and Genevra's heart sank. She hadn't meant to offend him. She just couldn't seem to keep her emotions under control. The strain of the last few days in coming to a decision, her preoccupation with Luke...she was in no fit state to carry on a business discussion.

'I'm sorry,' she sighed. 'I really am sorry, Mr Nemo. I don't expect you to understand...' She started to rise.

He stretched out a hand in protest, restraining any further movement. 'Please...please don't go. It seems to me that I'm the one who should be apologising. I beg you to forgive me for making you feel uncomfortable. It is...sometimes difficult . . . to meet a stranger. I was trying to put you at ease . . .' his grimace was full of savage irony ' . . . not drive you away. Could we start again?'

Genevra slowly nodded her agreement. She didn't know if she really wanted to stay. Christian Nemo was too disturbing a reminder of Luke. He had opened up the wounds of loving a man who was beyond her reach. She no longer cared about the commission he had in mind for her, but she couldn't turn her back on his appeal. It would be brutally insensitive after what she had said.

Christian Nemo resettled himself with an air of relief. 'May I call you Genevra?'

'Yes, of course,' she murmured.

'When I read your books on Devon and Cornwall, I knew you were the writer I wanted on this project. You did a splendid job of blending the right mixture of human interest with factual material.'

'Thank you.' It was incredibly difficult to focus her mind on to business. She felt as if she was split in two, one part of her accepting that Christian Nemo was a complete stranger, the other part in total conflict with such an acceptance. When she forced herself to speak, her voice sounded both defensive and aggressive.

'How did you happen to get hold of my books, Mr Nemo? They're only of local interest, and their distribution is very limited.'

'I was in Hampshire a couple of weeks ago, and I picked them up at a little village bookshop. I can't remember the name.'

The deep timbre of his voice struck a chord of recognition. The American accent was distracting, but it did not disguise the tonal quality that echoed out of Genevra's memory. Still, four years was a long time. Christian Nemo was built like Luke. It wasn't beyond the realms of possibility that his voice carried the same deep vibrancy.

Genevra made another effort to carry her end of the conversation. 'I must confess I've never heard of your publishing house, but then I'm barely acquainted with those in England. Do you publish a lot of tourist books?'

He smiled. 'They make up a good, constant market.'

That smile was so typical, so reminiscent— Genevra's heart leapt, then fell into an erratic pounding. Christian Nemo was driving her crazy, evoking memories of the man she loved. She studied his mouth as he talked—the shape of it, the way his lips moved, the occasional flash of white teeth— and she could see Luke talking just like that. She found herself wondering how she would react if those lips were to touch her own. Would they excite the same response? The thought jolted her so much that she barely heard Christian Nemo's series of statements, outlining the project he had in mind.

'What I envisage is a number of articles which will detail all that is of interest about the great historic country mansions and castles that have been converted to hotels. We'll do the best of them, the most unique and the most expensive.'

His voice gathered enthusiasm. 'Even if the readers can never afford to stay in such places, I want to give them the vicarious experience of doing so. Of course, your expenses will be paid, and we'll set an outright fee on each completed article. Besides that, you'll receive royalties on the book.'

Genevra was quite stunned by the offer. 'You mean, you actually want me to stay at these places so that I can write everything about them?'

'Of course.'

'And it won't cost me a thing?'

'Not in money. It will cost you time and effort.'

She was still digesting the proposition when a waiter arrived to ask their preference in tea, earnestly detailing the various types that were on offer. 'Darjeeling,' Genevra replied, automatically making the same choice that had sprung to her lips four years ago. The waiter departed, having received a nod of agreement from Christian Nemo.

'Can we do business together?' he asked.

It was a dream job, no doubt about it. An extraordinary offer to someone who was little more than an amateur author. Could she do credit to such a fantastic assignment? Christian Nemo apparently thought so, and why should she question his judgement? There was no reason for not trying her hand at it, and it certainly would be exciting to stay in such wonderful places, providing she could manage the trips away from home without compromising on what was really important to her.

She was not about to neglect her son. Auntie May adored Johnny and took wonderful care of him, but Genevra did not want to be a part-time mother. Nor could she expect her shop assistant, Beryl Parker, to manage the bookshop on her own for long periods of time. If Christian Nemo was in a hurry for a finished product, she couldn't possibly accept the job.

'Would I have to work to deadlines?' she asked, quickly adding, 'I do have other commitments that I can't ignore.'

'You can work at your own pace,' he assured her.

'How many places do you have in mind?'

'It's open-ended. Thirty...perhaps more... Really, it's up to you.'

'That will take a very long time,' Genevra warned.

'Yes. To do it properly would certainly take a long time.' The thought seemed to give him satisfaction. 'As I said before, I'm not concerned about time.' He hesitated a moment, then slowly added, 'There is one other thing...'

'Yes?'

His gaze held hers with steady deliberation. 'I want to see these places myself. I've already been to a couple in Hampshire. One of them—Chewton Glen—inspired the idea for this project. I'd like to follow through on the idea, and since I'm on convalescent leave for a few months, I intend to come with you. Call it self-indulgence. I hope you don't mind.'

Genevra struggled hard to conceal her dismay. To be closely associated with this man for months and months, sharing dinners and breakfasts across the same table, hours and hours of his company...haunting her with his smile...reminding her continually of the man she didn't have ... could she cope with it? Would familiarity gradually diminish the disturbing impact he had on her?

Her long hesitation prompted a sharp look of concern from Christian Nemo. 'I assure you, I'm not suggesting anything improper in this arrangement. I'm well aware that I'm not...' He clamped his mouth shut, and frowned in frustration.

Genevra was painfully reminded of the ultimatum she had delivered earlier. It seemed horribly ironic that he should think himself unattractive. The problem was that his likeness to Luke made him far too attractive for her peace of mind.

'I didn't think that,' she said quietly, and was grateful that the arrival of afternoon tea saved her from being pressed for an immediate decision. She needed more time to consider the position.

The tea service was all set out on the low table in front of them. Genevra accepted a couple of finger sandwiches, hoping they might help to settle her stomach. The tea was poured into their cups and, all too soon, Genevra was once more alone with Christian Nemo.

He looked at her expectantly and her heart quivered with indecision. As much as she wanted to take the job, being close to Christian Nemo, with his uncanny similarities to Luke, would surely constitute a form of self-torture that she would be stupid to invite upon herself. Yet she instinctively recoiled from saying anything that might hurt him, and she certainly didn't want him to take her rejection of his offer as a rejection of himself.

She sought for some tactful way out of the dilemma. 'How can you make such a project pay?' she asked. 'You'll never cover the costs.'

'I don't assess all my projects in purely dollar terms,' he replied drily. 'You have no need to worry about money.'

He was making it very difficult for her to refuse him. Genevra didn't know what to do. Then she thought of Johnny. No doubt Christian Nemo was expecting to move from one hotel to another, and she couldn't possibly do that.

'There is one difficulty, one that I might not be able to get over...'

He had been adding sugar to his tea. Very slowly and deliberately, he set the teaspoon down on the saucer. When he lifted his face to her, it was stripped of all expression. 'There's usually a way around most problems. If you'll tell me what's troubling you...'

'I'm not entirely free to do what you want, Mr Nemo,' she replied, her own careful expression softening as she thought of her son. 'I have a child. A little boy. And I can't...'

His teacup clattered across the table, dropped to the marble floor and smashed into a thousand fragments. Tea was splashed everywhere: over the scones, the butter, the jam-pots. Christian Nemo stood up as waiters descended on them.

His face was white and pained, the criss-crossing of scars showing up more sharply on the strained pallor of his skin. Not once did he look at Genevra while order was being restored, but his distress was so palpable that she felt her own nerves tighten. She didn't understand why such a simple, commonplace accident should upset him so much.

The waiters departed and Christian Nemo sat down again. Still he did not look at her. He stared down at his hands, the fingers of one stroking savagely over the other. 'Please excuse my clumsiness.

Occasionally I get a nerve spasm. Nothing I can do about it,' he said grimly.

'It doesn't matter,' Genevra sympathised.

But his distress did not ease. And it went deeper than distress. He was concealing it as best he could, but Genevra could feel his despair as if it was a tangible thing, crawling around her, tapping at her heart, and somehow it was a more frightening thing than anything she had ever experienced.

When he finally lifted his gaze to her, it was only for the most fleeting glance of acknowledgement. 'I didn't realise you were married. I should have asked before. Of course, the whole thing is impossible. I'm sorry for wasting your time.'

'I'm not married!'

His curt, clipped speech had somehow drawn the blunt retort from her. His head jerked up again, and Genevra coloured under the sharp reassessment.

'Unmarried mothers are not uncommon these days,' she said defensively.

'How old is the boy?' he rapped out, almost before she finished speaking.

'Johnny is three. Three and a half, to be exact.'

He looked as though she had slapped a brick in his face. To hell with him and his damned project, Genevra thought on a fierce surge of anger. If he thought any the less of her because she had Johnny, then she didn't want to do business with him, anyway.

'I'm sure you understand that a child needs his mother, and I consider his needs before anything else,' she said in belligerent defiance of any moral censure. 'I couldn't leave him for the length of time you're envisaging. So you're quite right, Mr Nemo. The whole thing is impossible!'

He gave a little shake of his head, and again he looked pained. 'You love him, Genevra?'

The soft, wistful question plunged her into confusion. The anger melted into a helpless vulnerability that wanted, needed his approval. 'Johnny is the best part of my life,' she blurted out, unconsciously revealing some of the loneliness of being a single parent.

The silence that followed her declaration held a strange stillness, like being in the eye of a storm. Genevra wondered why she didn't get up and go. Finish it. Yet she couldn't find the strength to make the break. Somehow, Christian Nemo held her tied to him with an emotional power that she didn't understand. If he had been Luke . . .

He suddenly smiled at her, and Genevra's heart turned over. 'Of course you must consider your son's welfare first,' he agreed warmly. 'But that's something we can get over, Genevra. We can arrange our schedule so that you needn't be away longer than one or two nights at a time. Do one

place a week, or every fortnight. Even do only one
a month, for that matter. And, if it's what you
want, we could take Johnny with us to the places
that would allow us to...'

He plunged on, answering every possible objec-
tion to her acceptance of his plans. Time didn't
matter to him; he was happy to wait on her con-
venience; he was sure he could spend the intervals
very pleasantly in St Ives; he liked children.

He was casting a net around her, leaving no
loophole for escape, and Genevra stared helplessly
at him, mesmerised by the mouth that was so like
Luke's. The turmoil pounded through her again,
urgently demanding answers that needed to be
settled. How would she cope with being put through
an emotional wringer every time she was in
Christian Nemo's company? Would it be different
the next time she saw him? Was it only the strain
of today that had her so hopelessly off balance?

She wanted to do the job. It was a marvellous
assignment, staying in all those exciting places and
writing about them. But if she committed
herself... what would she be committing herself to
in accepting such a close association with Christian
Nemo? If only there was some way of knowing...

'Are you happy with that arrangement?' he
asked.

Genevra's nerves prickled, sensing his need for
her acquiescence. Why was she so aware of him,

so sensitive to his feelings? She couldn't even bring herself to refuse him outright, despite her deep misgivings. The sense of something terribly important hanging in the balance was clouding her judgement, pressing her towards a course she knew could not be in her best interests...could it? She searched desperately for a compromise, and finally found one.

'Mr Nemo, you'll be spending a lot of money on this project, and I'm not sure I can deliver what you want. Before we start signing contracts or whatever, could we have a test run, so to speak? Go to one of these places—I'll pay my own way— and just see if I can satisfy your requirements. If not...'

'Certainly we can do that,' he declared, almost with an air of triumph, and again he took control, making arrangements so fast that Genevra had no time to reconsider.

He would pick her up from her hotel tomorrow afternoon, and they would stay overnight at the best hotel he could find at such short notice. Then he would see her safely home to St Ives the following day. As she agreed to this timetable, he visibly relaxed, but Genevra found her inner tension rising.

The decision had been made, for better or worse. She took her leave of Christian Nemo, feeling the oddest sensation that their lives were now inexorably intertwined, and there would be no escape. Ever.

If he had been Luke, coming back into her life, Genevra would not have questioned what she was feeling... but why was she reacting so strongly to a total stranger?

# CHAPTER FOUR

NONE of the famous London landmarks made any impression whatsoever on Genevra as the taxi wove through the afternoon traffic. The trip to her hotel was blurred by wave after wave of chaotic emotion, and all of them swirled around the enigma of Christian Nemo.

She had been so certain he was Luke. It seemed impossible that two men could be so alike. Not the face—she couldn't refute the cruel evidence of those altered features—but all the rest: his physique, the smile, the deep timbre of his voice, even the touch of his hand had felt like Luke's.

It was madness to keep going over it all, yet Genevra could no more control her thoughts than she had been able to control her reactions to Christian Nemo. Not once in all these years of waiting for Luke had any man caused so much as a flutter in Genevra's heart, let alone played havoc with it. Even now, her pulse was racing at the thought of being with him tomorrow. And tomorrow night. And the next day.

Only Luke had ever . . . only Luke!

It *was* him!

It *had* to be!

The taxi pulled up at her hotel, and Genevra stepped out, sternly telling herself to get her feet back on the ground. She had to be wrong. Christian Nemo had flatly denied being Luke when they had first met. He talked like an American. His eye colour was different.

She recited those facts over to herself as she went up to her room, but she could not dispel the power of that wild idea. It kept growing, gathering force, taking over her mind. They had to be one and the same person! Surely it was the only answer that made sense of what she was feeling.

Madness, her mind screamed, but her heart beat a jubilant tattoo, and every instinct in her body played clarions of approval, drowning out the shrill voice of reason. And with all the force of her being Genevra commanded herself to forget Christian Nemo's face and the wrong eye colour, forget the American accent and everything else that couldn't be explained away. Somewhere there was an explanation. Had to be!

The meeting at the Dorchester, it was no coincidence at all. Luke would have chosen that venue to meet her again...at the same table they had shared before!

And her recognition of him had been instant and certain! She had felt no hesitation or confusion until he had turned around, and even then her instincts had still insisted it was Luke. There could be no doubt at all about the way he had made her feel.

But why would he pretend to be someone else? What motivation could he possibly have to play such a heartless game with her? Did he think she might not love him after all this time...or might not love the man he had become? Genevra found that a sobering thought.

She kicked off her shoes, hung up her suit-coat, then flopped down on the bed, intent on focusing her whole concentration on the problem.

Maybe he didn't feel he could present himself as the man who had swept her off her feet four years ago. He had been very, very conscious of the injuries to his face. And what other injuries had he sustained? Genevra wondered, remembering the walking-cane, the stiffness of his left leg when he sat down, and the nerve spasm in his hand. Another, even more pertinent thought sped into Genevra's mind...how long had all that corrective surgery taken?

What if Luke had lied to her in that letter, four years ago? What if he had been in some terrible accident soon after returning to Australia, had been disfigured, perhaps even partially paralysed, with little prospect of ever leading the kind of life he had wanted with her? Might he not have backed off from the marriage they had planned, deliberately cutting her free from any sense of obligation to him?

'I could not be happy within myself, nor could I make you happy... It will be best for both of us to try and forget what could have been...'

The words he had written leapt out of Genevra's memory, taking on a new meaning.

How many operations had he suffered through in order to emerge as the man who had introduced himself as Christian Nemo? And the project... surely that was simply a plan to spend time with her, to see if it was possible to recapture the love they had once shared. If such was the case, the money wouldn't mean anything to him, nor the time. And he would make every accommodation in the world to fit in with the son he hadn't known he had.

Johnny! The teacup knocked flying... she had just begun to tell him that she had a child. The shock, his pain and agitation, and then the despair she had sensed when he had thought she was married... now she understood! And her heart wept tears of blood for him.

His life—the life he had so painfully reconstructed—had been hanging on her answer, and she had been so close, so terribly close to turning her back on the future she had been waiting for all these years. She could well imagine the uncertainties that had racked him, forcing him to adopt the measures he had. He wasn't to know she still loved him, and *would* love him, no matter how he looked or what had happened to him.

She had to show him, reassure him, convince him, wipe any uncertainty out of his mind! A fierce exultation swept through Genevra's body. Tomorrow couldn't come fast enough. Her mind filled with all sorts of exciting plans.

She had time to go shopping in the morning. She would go to Harrods and be wildly extravagant. Matthew had urged her to spend some of the trust money on herself, and what better purpose could it be used for than pursuing her one chance for happiness? She wanted to look beautiful for Luke. She had to make him see that she found him as desirable as ever, that she wanted to attract his desire, that nothing could change her love for him.

A tiny bell of caution rang across her fevered thoughts. What if she was wrong? What if Christian Nemo was exactly what he said he was...an American publisher?

No! Everything within her heaved an instant rebellion against any doubt. She was not going to let herself be confused again. Not even the colour of his eyes could change her mind.

And yet...how could she explain that away? The colour of people's eyes didn't change. Not from grey to brown. It was inexplicable.

But that didn't matter. There had to be some explanation, because Genevra was now certain that she was right. Whatever the consequences to herself, she was going to act on that unalterable certainty, and somehow she would prove that Christian Nemo and Luke Stanford were one and the same person.

Positive action, that was what she had vowed to herself before approaching Matthew this afternoon. Genevra wished she had gone to him weeks before. Then she wouldn't have had to rely on her intuition. She would have had confirmation of Luke's accident. But she couldn't wait for that now. There had to be a quicker way to prove Luke's identity and force him to reveal the truth.

The mole! No two men could have exactly the same mole, and she remembered precisely where it was...remembered lying in bed with him, her fingers lightly brushing over it just below the pit of his back. All she had to do was get him to undress!

Well, she could always seduce him, Genevra thought on a mad wave of positive thinking; then softly laughed at herself. She was no *femme fatale*, practised in the art of seduction. There had only ever been Luke for her, and what had happened between them had simply happened because they both wanted it so much.

A ripple of remembered pleasure coursed through her body, and Genevra hugged it tightly to herself, wanting it to last, wanting to capture it again. It had been so long...so long since she had lain in Luke's arms, sharing all the wonderful intimacies of loving.

Surely he craved it, too? If she touched him, he would have to respond, just as he had always done. And if she dressed up for him, showed him in her manner and speech that nothing had changed for her, how could he resist the temptation she would offer him?

The need for his loving, her own need to love him was an ache that urgently demanded some appeasement. And what better way of proving to him that he was the man she wanted? She would make it up to him for all he had suffered to come back to her, show him that nothing else mattered but having him with her again. A blissful contentment spread through her, bringing relaxation for the first time in many days.

A small worm of sanity insisted that if Christian Nemo was truly Christian Nemo, and not Luke Stanford, she was about to make the most disastrous mistake of her life, but she swept the thought aside. She was not going to be a passive victim of her emotions any longer. She had made her decision and nothing...*nothing* was going to shift her from it.

Yves Saint Laurent—never in her life had Genevra worn a designer-label outfit, but as she slipped the top on over the brilliantly striped skirt, and admired the total effect, she thought it would be very easy to become addicted to buying such wonderful clothes.

She felt more vibrantly alive than she had done in years, and vibrant was certainly the key-word, she thought with a delighted grin. The skirt and matching top featured brilliant bands of fuchsia-pink, red, orange, violet, green and turquoise, as well as black and white; and the beautifully set white collar on the low V-neckline of the sleeveless top was the crowning touch of class.

Not to mention the Christian Dior sandals! The soft leather cross-over straps were the same marvellous shade of fuchsia-pink as in the dress, and the black button at the side of the ankle-strap and the black high heels lent a very sexy elegance to the design.

A warm tingle of excitement brought a glowing colour to Genevra's cheeks. She didn't look pale and pinched today. Her blue eyes were sparkling with happy anticipation, and her whole face seemed to have acquired a youthful bloom overnight. She felt like dancing on top of the world and shouting out to everyone that the man she loved had come back to her.

And she was ready for him now! Genevra's gaze fell exultantly on all the shopping bags strewn over the bed in her hotel room. She had spent an absolute fortune, over a thousand pounds, but the outlay was well worth every penny if she could make Luke drop his pose of being a stranger. And if the dress she had bought for tonight didn't spark off a desire to make love to her, then he would have to be made of iron!

Genevra checked her watch. It was still twenty minutes short of two o'clock, twenty minutes before Luke... She had to remember to call him Christian Nemo until he admitted his true identity.

Genevra packed the new clothes into her suitcase and dispensed with the shopping-bags, then, feeling a little guilty about her uncharacteristic extravagance, she rang Matthew to warn him that a large account would be coming in to be paid from the trust fund. She had never done such a thing before but, when she confessed her spending spree to Matthew, his oft-repeated comment of 'Splendid!' expressed a ringing approval that satisfactorily cleared her conscience.

Anticipation lightened her step as she went down to the reception desk to pay her hotel bill. The clerk behind the desk cast a frankly appreciative eye over her, and Genevra's heart gave a skip of elated triumph. She really did look good! She was still smiling over his very courteous attention when the Silver Cloud Rolls-Royce pulled up outside the hotel entrance.

Genevra stared in surprise as Luke stepped out of it. Christian Nemo, she swiftly corrected herself. She hadn't expected him to travel in that degree of luxury, although the kind of hotels he had described for the project would certainly be catering to people of the highest wealth-bracket. Did a construction business generate that kind of money? Then she remembered that Luke had flown first-class from England to Australia. She simply hadn't realised how well off he was.

She turned towards him as he entered the hotel foyer and her heart did more than skip a beat when he stopped dead in his tracks and stared at her. Several pulse-galloping moments passed before he took a deep breath and moved forwards, holding out his hand to her.

'I thought you beautiful yesterday, Genevra,' he said in a deep, husky voice. 'But today...'

The intensity of his gaze choked the breath in Genevra's throat. She existed only for him as he slowly took in the sparkling blue of her eyes, the becoming flush of colour in her cheeks, the shiny ripple of black waves falling to her shoulders, the soft fullness of her mouth.

'...but today you look ravishing,' he finished softly.

His hand curled around hers, subtly pressing an ownership that she gladly gave up to him. 'Thank you,' she all but whispered, then laughed out of sheer happiness. 'I thought I'd better dress up to the assignment.'

He laughed too, and it was the strongest possible echo of the past when he replied, 'Dress doesn't matter.' His smile curled around Genevra's heart as he added, 'But I feel very privileged to have your company, and I hope you'll enjoy your stay at Le Manoir aux Quat'Saisons.'

He tucked her hand around his arm, directed the clerk to get the suitcase carried to the car, then led Genevra outside and handed her into the Rolls-Royce. It looked like the same car that she had seen arriving at the Dorchester Hotel yesterday afternoon, and Genevra decided that it probably was, since Luke had only been a minute or two ahead of her.

She watched him covertly as he settled back into the seat beside her.

He was less formally dressed today, but the light grey trousers, white shirt and navy blazer were still conservative, as was the tasteful grey tie with its thin red, white and navy stripes. She remembered Luke's love of sporty, casual clothes, and wondered if his taste had really changed. Not that it mattered to her.

'Do you always motor around in a Rolls-Royce?' she asked curiously.

'No, only in England. I need a chauffeured car here.' He turned his head slightly away from her so that the black eye-patch was hidden from her sight before adding, 'I have a problem judging distances with only one eye, and I can't get an international driver's licence.'

'I don't mind, you know,' Genevra said softly.

A dry smile curved his mouth. 'Not many people do mind riding in such cars.'

'I didn't mean that. I meant the scars and whatever else you feel you have to hide,' she said in a rush, sensing an emotional retreat from her and anxious to stop it.

'Why do you think I've got something to hide?'

His sharp frown warned her that she was going too fast, and Genevra instantly back-pedalled. 'You spoke yesterday of choosing that table at the Dorchester so as to be out of view of the people there. I just want you to know that I don't find the view of your face at all offensive. Quite the contrary, in fact. So please don't turn away from me.'

He probed the sincerity in her eyes for a long moment before giving a bemused little shake of his head. 'Are you always this direct?'

'I would like you to be direct with me,' she retorted fearlessly.

He sliced her a slightly guarded look. 'What do you want to know?'

'You must have been in a frightful accident,' she prompted. 'Do you mind telling me what happened?'

He did not reply immediately, and she could feel him closing up, even before he spoke. 'Morbid curiosity?'

She flushed at the implied reprimand. 'I'm sorry. If you prefer not to talk about it...'

'I much prefer,' he answered curtly.

Genevra bit her tongue and stared at the back of the chauffeur's head as he started the car and steered it smoothly into a stream of traffic. She had blundered again, too eager to fill in the lost years. The craving to know all that had happened to him was hard to repress.

On the other hand, she could understand that Luke had no desire to recall a time that must have been terribly painful, both physically and mentally. She was an insensitive fool to have mentioned it. Wasn't it enough that he was here with her now?

But she would like to know if she was right about his letter, that it was the accident which had forced him into denying her, and not marriage to another woman.

'Is there anything else?' he asked in a matter-of-fact tone that effectively cut through the tense silence which had fallen between them.

Genevra's relief at the opening he had given her was almost instantly checked by the realisation that he might be offended again if he thought she was questioning his sense of morality. She tried a more indirect approach.

'If I'm to be with you, staying at hotels, there are some things I need to know...'

'Go on,' he urged as she hesitated.

Genevra took a deep breath and plunged on. 'Well, you made the point with me yesterday, so I think it's fair to ask you...' She turned to meet his gaze, and found the same guarded expression she had seen before. 'Are you married?' she asked point-blank.

A fleeting look of sadness accompanied his brief answer. 'Not any more.'

Somehow, Genevra covered up her shock, nodding an acknowledgement of the reply before turning her gaze back to the chauffeur's head. As hurt welled over the shock, she looked out the side window, pretending an interest in their route.

Not any more...so what was he? Divorced? Widowed? And why the look of sadness? The fact of the marriage hurt badly enough, although he had spelled it out to her in the letter. But the sadness! Why should he feel sad about the end of a marriage he hadn't wanted? Or did he feel sad because he had been forced to hurt her with his marriage to another woman?

The squeeze on Genevra's heart eased a little. 'I know too well the pain it will give you——' that was what he had written '—and wish with all my heart that I did not have to make this choice...'

Maybe it was the accident—his injuries—that had brought about the end of the marriage. Whatever had happened, he was free now. That was the important thing. And he had come back to her. Nothing else really mattered.

'Genevra . . .'

It was a soft appeal for her attention and, feeling once more in command of herself, Genevra had no hesitation in turning back to him. 'Yes?'

'I would not compromise you in any way. Please don't doubt that,' he said seriously. 'If you ever feel I'm imposing on your time, and you'd prefer to be by yourself . . .'

She reached over to touch his arm in a quick, reassuring gesture. 'But I'm very happy for us to be together,' she said; then, seeing his surprise, she quickly added, 'I need all the help you can give me. How else will I know exactly what you want?'

His smile was slow in coming, but it spilled an exultant joy into Genevra's heart. 'I'm glad you see it that way.'

Her own smile held all the love that had always been his. 'Tell me about this place we're going to. I don't even know where it is.'

The air of tense reserve completely disappeared. He relaxed and spoke in a tone of happy anticipation. 'It's in Oxfordshire. We should be there in under an hour. The Manoir is actually situated in the village of Great Milton, just five miles from

Oxford. The building is mainly an eighteenth-century manor house, but its origins go back to the fourteenth century. The Egon Ronay Guide gives the hotel a de-luxe rating and the restaurant three stars—one of the finest in Britain. The wine list is outstanding...'

Genevra watched him talk. She listened, too, nodding and smiling in all the right places, asking questions about the hotel that had impressed him so much in Hampshire, Chewton Glen.

He recalled all the details that he thought were pertinent to his concept of the project. Genevra actually began to wonder if Luke had left construction work and gone into publishing since his accident. But it was the way he was responding to her that held most of her attention.

He forgot about his face and, as Genevra got used to the altered features, she decided that the surgeon had done a masterly job. The altered nose was the right shape to balance the jawline. The barely visible scars were obviously the result of skin-grafts, and would probably fade altogether in time.

Luke was just as handsome as he had always been, although in a different way. The tawny-brown eye colour was quite startlingly attractive with his dark eyelashes and hair. She wondered if he was wearing a contact lens. Was it possible to get tinted ones? There had to be some answer to the puzzle.

She loved his smile. Loved all of him with a passion that could hardly wait for tonight. He was trying to hold back, to keep up his role of being a stranger, but Genevra knew she was wearing the barriers down. She could feel the rapport creeping back, that same magic rapport that had leapt between them four years ago.

Twice his gaze clung to hers while he forgot what he had been saying, and she sensed his need and his incredulity at the need that she was projecting. Each time, he gave a slight shake of his head before distractedly resuming the line of conversation that had been left hanging.

The third time, he actually jerked his head away and she saw his hand clench. Genevra was certain that he had wanted to reach out and touch her. 'We're coming into Great Milton now,' he announced, and the strained note in his voice was like a chord of beautiful music to Genevra's ears. She didn't doubt for one moment that he wanted her as much as ever, and the restraint he was forcing upon himself could not last long, particularly if she applied some real pressure.

Great Milton was a pretty village, more picturesque than most, with the well-kept neatness of its thatched cottages spread around the village green. Luke half leaned across her to point out the almost perfect symmetry of one cottage: chimneys at each end of the thatched roof, attic windows positioned directly above the windows on either side of the central door, window-boxes with identical flowers, and matching pot-plants hanging just under the eaves.

Genevra nodded her appreciation, but she was far more conscious of the nearness of Luke's body. His blazer had fallen open, and she could almost feel the warmth of his broad chest. All she had to do was turn towards him and she would virtually be within the circle of his arms. But before she could act on the temptation, he drew back and the moment was gone. She found herself clenching her own hands as she fought to calm her disordered pulse.

A leafy lane took them to a very old village church with a clock tower. Its high stone walls extended to the impressive gateway of the Manoir.

'Here we are.' His fingers lightly brushed her forearm, as if he could no longer resist the impulse to touch her.

However, his gaze was rather pointedly fixed on the grounds they were entering, and Genevra could not make anything positive out of the light contact. Reluctantly, she turned her attention to the subject she was supposed to write about.

The driveway was lined with trees and garden beds that were ablaze with yellow violas. On the beautifully kept lawn to their right were tables and chairs of white aluminium lace, shaded by bright pink umbrellas. The chauffeur turned the Rolls-Royce into the spacious, gravelled courtyard that fronted the stately manor house, and parked it near the entrance doorway which was framed with climbing roses.

Genevra could not disguise her own air of heightened excitement as Christian Nemo helped her to alight from the car. He took her by the arm, drawing her close to him, and she had no doubt that his need to feel her body next to his was as uncontrollable as her own. It was no longer a matter of her seducing him, but of how long they would have to wait before they were alone together.

They walked into a rather small reception room, but Genevra noted it was strikingly furnished with antiques, and the floral arrangements were nothing short of magnificent. Conscious that their sexual tension might be all too evident to the receptionist, Genevra deliberately feasted her eyes on everything else while Christian spoke to the woman.

'I've given Miss Kingsley the Hollyhock Room. You're in Hydrangea, Mr Nemo,' the receptionist announced, then added with a touch of pride, 'All our rooms are named after flowers and decorated accordingly. I hope you'll both enjoy your stay here.'

A porter took Genevra's suitcase and led the way upstairs. At the top landing, he indicated that the Hydrangea Room was up a few more stairs at the end of the hallway, then turned in the opposite direction to show them to the Hollyhock Room.

Genevra felt a stab of disappointment at the distance between the two rooms, but she quickly dismissed the idea that any distance could keep them apart now.

When the porter opened her door and invited Genevra to step inside, she hastened forwards, impatient for the formalities to be over. However, her first glance at the room left her absolutely stunned.

Its luxurious size, the superb elegance of its furnishings, the sheer marvellous richness of everything drew her forwards in gaping wonder.

She heard the porter say something about bringing up the other suitcases, but Genevra was so entranced by what was in front of her that she didn't notice his departure. She had seen pictures of fantastic bedroom suites, but the reality was almost too much to take in.

The double bed looked fabulous with its ornamental canopy hanging from the wall above it. The use of the hollyhock fabric, with its sprays of flowers scalloped by a print of blue ribbon, was the touch of a brilliant decorator. The side-drapes from the canopy were complemented by a tightly gathered central drape of hollyhock-pink silk. The bedhead and quilt were padded in the floral fabric, while the valance around the base of the bed repeated the pink silk. At least half a dozen white lace pillows were piled up in front of the bedhead.

And the bed was only the start!

A four-seater Louis the fourteenth sofa, upholstered in blue silk, graced the window position in front of the wide stretch of hollyhock curtains. There were two wing-backed armchairs in pink silk, a coffee-table, a writing-table with a matching Chippendale chair, another table draped with a white lace cloth on which stood a complimentary bowl of fruit, two elegant dining-chairs, a beautifully polished antique chest of drawers, a cheval-glass, paintings on the walls, graceful lamps...

'Like it?'

She turned sparkling eyes back to Christian Nemo. 'I love it!'

He was smiling indulgently at her. 'This must be the bathroom,' he said, moving towards a door on the left of the entrance.

In a burst of pleasurable anticipation, Genevra whirled back and hugged his arm as he opened the door.

The bathroom was perfectly matched to the bedroom décor. Even the thick beige carpet extended inside, and the mirror above the vanity bench was surrounded by a padded frame of the hollyhock fabric. The tiles were a pearly-pink, and the bath, basin and shower all had gold fittings. A potted palm sat on a ledge above the bath, and beautiful dishes held Lancôme toilette products.

'This is positively decadent,' Genevra breathed.

Christian Nemo gave a soft laugh which abruptly stopped as she looked up at him. She saw the sharp conflict between desire and caution, felt the muscle in his arm tighten under her touch. As of one accord, they turned to each other. Genevra's hand feathered up the lapel of his blazer, ready to curl around his neck. He gripped her waist, fingers sliding around to draw her closer.

There was a knock on the door!

'Mr Nemo?'

His fingers suddenly dug into her flesh, forcibly halting their encircling progress. His head jerked up. 'Yes?' he replied on a swiftly indrawn breath.

'I've brought your bags up, sir. Would you like to be shown to your room now?'

'Yes. Thank you,' he clipped out, and in a stiff, defensive move, he held Genevra still as he stepped back from her, and only when he had put some distance between them did he meet the urgent plea in her eyes.

But he didn't answer it! To her hurt bewilderment, he even pretended not to see it. Somehow, he had managed to pull a mask of formality over his own feelings and, when he spoke, his voice projected a flat denial of anything explosive between them.

'I'll leave you to settle in, Genevra. Give you time to really look around and enjoy what's here. Perhaps in an hour or so you'd like to walk around the grounds. Take everything in.'

'Yes. Yes, I would like that,' she murmured, feeling completely deflated by his withdrawal.

'Fine. I'll call by your door then.'

'Fine,' she echoed.

And he left her without a backward glance, his gait stiff, his shoulders decisively squared.

Genevra felt so frustrated that she almost slammed the door after him. He needn't have gone, she thought angrily. He could have told the porter to put the bags in his room and leave the key in the door. Why, why, why had he turned away from her like that?

She paced the floor, trying to fathom his reasons, totally uncaring of the luxury around her. Was he still unsure of how she felt about him? Was he afraid of a rebuff if he went too fast? He had sworn not to compromise her in any way; did he feel honour-bound not to take advantage of the situation?

Genevra shook her head, not knowing what to think. But one way or another, she would crack open that façade of control before tonight was over.

As far as she was concerned, the waiting was a thing of the past. This man wanted her and she wanted him. Genevra was certain who he was, and she was not going to let anything stand in the way of their coming together.

# CHAPTER FIVE

THE man who called himself Christian Nemo came to her room an hour later. He wore an air of reserve.

Genevra gave him the full brilliance of her smile, closed her door, and slid her hand around his. There was a momentary passivity, then almost convulsively his fingers closed around hers.

She chattered gaily to him on their way downstairs; not giving him a chance to be at all sober or serious; and once outside she effervesced with happy enthusiasm over everything in sight. He relaxed. He smiled. He laughed. He looked at her as if he wanted to devour all that she offered him.

And dancing through Genevra's mind was an exultant refrain... "He's mine, mine, mine! And no one else can ever have him from now on."

The surrounds of the Manoir were fascinating: paths cutting through manicured lawns and bordered by wonderful rose-gardens; magnificent trees; shrubs shaped by the art of topiary; flowering vines dressing the old stone walls; a splendid, if somewhat crumbling dovecote; picturesque outbuildings that had once housed carriages, but which now contained service rooms for the hotel; an enclosed swimming pool surrounded by the now-familiar white furniture and pink umbrellas; and beyond the immediate environs were twenty-seven acres of country fields and the chef's extensive kitchen garden.

It was an exhilarating walk, every step forging a more intense awareness of each other. They saw other guests enjoying the peaceful beauty of the grounds. They even talked to a couple of gardeners, pretending an interest in the contents of the igloo hot-houses. But all the words they spoke and all the walking they did was just a game, a marvellous game of driving anticipation to its most exquisite limits.

When it was time to dress for dinner, Genevra parted from Luke at the top of the staircase, almost skipping away from him in teasing provocation— wanting to dress up for him, wanting to drive him out of his mind with desire so that there could never, never be any turning away, wanting it to be the most magical night of their lives. And she was pulsatingly aware of the yearning that emanated from him as he watched her go.

She sang in the shower. She made lavish use of the Lancôme products. She deliberately dispensed with wearing a bra. She felt deliciously, wickedly wanton as she twirled around in the new dress, assessing its sexiness in the cheval-glass.

It was a beautiful dress, predominantly pink, but patterned with streaks of white and two shades of blue. The full, graceful three-quarter-length sleeves were in a matching fabric, with deeper shades of the same colours, as were the inset gores of the lovely swinging skirt. A wide, elasticised waistband accentuated the curves of her figure. A scalloped satin-stitch of the two shades of blue featured the low V-neckline, and from the neck-edge of the shoulder seam fell string ties ending in silk tassles, which, when tied loosely at the base of her throat, added the classy touch that dispensed with any need for jewellery.

Genevra's blue eyes sparkled with delight at her reflection. The dress was not overtly sexy, but it certainly showed off the fact that she was a woman, and the silky sensuousness of the softly flowing fabric made her feel very physically aware of herself. She lifted a hand and ran it experimentally over the thrusting fullness of her breasts, and felt her nipples leaping into hard prominence.

Rampant thoughts on how Luke would touch her tonight sent ripples of excitement through her body. She couldn't think of him as Christian Nemo. Besides, after tonight there would be no need to. After they had made love and she had found the mole which would prove his identity, the truth had to come out. And then they would make love again in the full knowledge of each other and . . .

When his knock came, Genevra's breathing had already become ragged from her feverish imaginings. She opened the door and almost melted on the spot as he stared at her, speechless, the quick rise and fall of his chest revealing his own sexual tension.

'Genevra...' It was a whisper of hungry, compelling desire. His gaze lifted to hers, glazed with need. 'Tell me this is not a game with you. Tell me I'm not imagining this...'

'It's no game. And it's as real as it ever was...' She barely stopped herself from calling him Luke. Not yet. Not until he admitted it, she cautioned herself.

He shook his head, trying to break the spell of desire that bound them together. 'You hardly know me.'

'I know you as well as you know me,' she reminded him.

Painful doubt looked back at her. 'I didn't think...didn't expect...'

'Because it's been so long?' she asked softly, then stepped forwards, reaching up to caress the faintly lined cheek. 'Or because of this?'

'Don't!' It was a hoarse, explosive whisper. He plucked her hand away, as if he couldn't bear her touch. His fingers worked over hers in extreme agitation. 'It's too soon! I can't risk losing control and spoiling our relationship at this early stage. Don't tempt me, Genevra. We need...to know each other better. To talk...about things.'

A happy triumph burst through her. He was going to confess his real identity! 'Then let's go down to dinner and talk.'

Her amenability to his need for more time brought a short laugh of sheer relief. 'God knows how I'm going to do the meal justice with you sitting across from me! You're the most terrible temptation any man could have, Genevra.'

'But there's only one man I want,' she said, and her eyes quite blatantly declared her desire for him.

He made no reply to her assertion until they were seated in the dining-room and served with champagne and a platter of appetisers. He looked at her over his glass of wine, his gaze drifting down the rippling cascade of shiny black hair, skating over the jutting fullness of her breasts, then finally met the unflinching directness of her eyes.

'You were right upstairs. It has been a long time since I've been with...or even wanted to be with a woman. And the truth is, you affect me in a way no other woman has ever affected me. I would do anything for you.'

Beautiful, marvellous, glorious words that Genevra revelled in. 'It seems I've been waiting for ever for you,' she murmured fervently. 'Don't make me wait any longer.'

'Genevra...' A look of anguish crossed his face. 'I didn't come prepared for...for this contingency.

I don't want you...conceiving a child that's not planned.'

'I'm older and wiser now,' she replied softly, understanding the guilt he obviously felt over Johnny, and loving him all the more for his caring. 'It can't happen tonight,' she assured him, and silently vowed to see her doctor as soon as she got back to St Ives. There would be time for another baby in the future, but not too soon. Johnny deserved to have his father's sole attention for a while.

She smiled as she sensed his relief. With it came the slow release of the restraint he had been tightly holding on to, but he did not smile back at her. The accelerated pulse of his emotion was too strong for smiling.

'Tell me about your life...your son. I want to know everything about you,' he commanded, need throbbing behind every word.

He meant the lost years, Genevra thought, and for a moment the pain of separation that he had inflicted on both of them held her tongue. She wanted him to tell her the full truth about his marriage, the accident, all that had happened to him; but then she realised that such topics could only bring them both pain, whereas telling him about his son would give them pleasure.

She told him everything she could think of about Johnny's childhood, and not for one moment did he look the slightest bit bored with the subject. He listened with rapt attention, encouraged her into more and more detail, seemingly enthralled by her relationship with her son. The son he should have shared with her, Genevra thought sadly. But he was sharing now! What point was there in regretting time that had gone when she had now?

The meal was superb: a terrine of *bouillabaisse* with fennel, baby leeks and virgin olive oil; tender fillet of lamb, fanned into a central rosette and served with perfect baby turnips, snow peas, peeled broad beans and small circles of crisped potato; then a lemon soufflé, so light and delicate that it vanished in the mouth.

The setting was elegant, the service impeccable, the French wine as smooth as silk; all contributing an extra edge of magic to this night of nights. But best of all for Genevra was the feeling of being where she belonged, with Luke, sharing all that could be shared.

With each minute that passed, the need to touch grew stronger. It wasn't enough to talk or to look or to even hold hands, which only fed the desire for greater intimacy. Coffee and *petits fours* were served and ignored by both of them. They couldn't tear their eyes off each other. Silence fell between them, a silence that grew tense with unfulfilled passion.

'Do you want this coffee?' he asked, a rough edge furring his voice.

'No,' she breathed through a sudden constriction in her throat.

He stood up, stepping quickly to hold her chair for her. Genevra's thighs quivered in anticipation as she rose to take his arm. Neither of them spoke a word as they walked up to her room. The door shut the rest of the world out.

He tore off his jacket as she reached for him. He gathered her hard to him, her breasts crushed to the thundering beat of his chest, her lower body thrust into a more urgently pulsing hardness. Their mouths sought a swifter means of mutual possession, their fierce kiss initiating an erotic prelude for what was to come: tasting, teasing, tangling with an avid need for the passionate mingling of flesh, wildly hungry for every exciting nuance of intimacy.

Her hands were raking up his back, thrusting into his hair, then dragging down to close convulsively over his tight buttocks as she arched into him. He wrenched his mouth from hers, groaning his need. His voice held a hoarse, driven sound as he gasped, 'I can't wait, Genevra.'

'I don't want you to,' she breathed, exulting in her power to arouse him beyond his control, wanting to give him the pleasure that would ease his pain and bring them both the ultimate peace of total union.

His hands slid down her thighs and gathered up her skirt as his mouth claimed hers again. His fingers grazed up to the bare skin of her stomach, pushed under the band of her wispy lace panties and peeled them down, making her flesh leap with excitement at his every touch. He reached for the fever-heated apex between her thighs, caressing her with a delicate pressure that sent quivers of pleasure-shock through her whole body. Her knees buckled. An iron-tight arm held her pinned to him as he moved her to the bed and quickly disposed of her shoes and panties.

She reached for him, but her fingers were weak, boneless, merely brushing down the swollen hardness of his erection. His stomach contracted with tension. His gaze glittered over her as he threw off his tie and attacked the buttons of his shirt. Somehow, she found the strength to push herself up and lift her dress over her head. He straightened from removing his trousers and she flung her arms around his waist, pressing her cheek to the moist nakedness of his heaving chest.

'God almighty!' It was a tremulous gasp.

'You're mine now. Mine!' she said fiercely, and her lips pressed her claim in a sensuous trail of kisses.

'Genevra!' The cry echoed with years of aching need. He arched back, the powerful thrust of his manhood sliding through the soft valley of her breasts. His hands gripped her under her arms and lifted, hauling her up for his mouth to ravage hers as he carried her with him down on to the pillows.

He smothered her face with kisses, punctuating them with hoarse words of wild adoration. He shaped her breasts to his mouth and sucked on them as if he would draw the very essence from her soul. The most exquisite pleasure spurted through her, making her writhe and arch in uninhibited abandonment to all he would do to her.

He caressed her legs apart, his fingers delving into the intimate crevices and manipulating a sensitivity that drove her beyond madness. She felt her inner muscles convulsing out of control, and almost wept with relief as he pushed into her, a hot, heavy fullness that made her tremble with ecstatic satisfaction. Her hands shot down to drag at his powerful thighs, pulling him deeper. Her legs instinctively curled around his, lifting herself up to him, urging that final devastating plunge that took him all the way into her womb.

And that sensation eclipsed all others, the feel of him at the centre of her being, possessing and possessed. His hands curved around her buttocks, supporting her there with him, of him, together. She opened her eyes and it was Luke's body hovering above hers: beautiful, strong, a streamlined symphony of taut flesh and muscle, sheened with the heat of their desire for each other.

She lifted a limp hand and stroked a sensual line from belly to groin. He shuddered and unleashed a fiery rhythm of stroking thrusts that drove electric tingles into every cell of her body, fusing them into a sweet, aching sea of pleasure-pain that swelled to a climactic crest and crashed into pure bliss.

And still there was the exquisite movement inside her, faster, faster, spilling her into wave after wave of glorious sensation, and the ultimate spasms of his climax brought the final intense fulfilment of all the dreams she had ever had. He toppled forwards and she caught him to her, hugging him with all the love in her heart, pressing soft little kisses to his throat and cheek, until he lifted his head to sweep her mouth with his own in a tender salute of love.

'You know what I'm thinking?' he smiled down at her.

'Tell me,' she murmured, her eyes shining with a languorous happiness.

'I'm the luckiest man alive. And even now, I don't know why or how, only that I am.'

'Because you're you,' she replied, loving his smile, loving everything about him.

He stroked her hair, fanning the long tresses out on the pillow. 'Are you a sorceress, Genevra?'

She laughed up at him. 'I only have magic for you.'

'I want it to go on and on,' he said with serious fervour. 'Do you want that, too?'

'For ever,' she breathed, her need for him glittering in her eyes as she wound her arms around his neck and pulled his head down to hers.

Their kiss held no urgent passion, but it awakened a purely sensual desire to touch and taste each other in less frantic haste. They found a beautifully erotic delight in pleasuring with caresses and kisses, savouring every intimate knowledge gained and greedy for more.

Like seasoned partners in a primitive pagan ritual, they moved around each other; exciting, soothing, teasing, building slowly to the final mating ceremony, which they performed with a restrained, sensual deliberation, heightening every fragmented awareness of sliding together, becoming one, again and again and again until they could not bear the control any longer, their need exploding into a barbaric wildness that left them both exhausted and totally sated.

Then they lay in each other's arms, too drained to speak or move, knowing there were no words or actions left that could express the sense of belonging that bound them together. Nothing could have been more total, more complete.

Genevra listened contentedly to the soft sigh of her lover's breathing, and knew he was at peace. The long separation was over, and they would never be parted again. Her hand glided down his back in a wholly possessive caress, and it was only then that she remembered about the mole.

She smiled to herself. As if she needed proof now! It wasn't possible that two different men could draw such a basic response from her.

There was no question in her mind as her hand continued its downward slide. She knew him so intimately that the mole merely represented another small dimension of familiarity. Her fingers lightly swept the area of skin near the pit of his back, seeking the different texture she knew was there.

She couldn't find it. She concentrated more carefully on the task, willing her fingertips to detect what had to be detected. But there was no different texture, no change at all in the pattern of his smooth flesh, not even when she searched further afield, in case she had forgotten the exact position.

The man lying in her arms, intimately entwined with her...the man to whom she had just given herself body and soul...did not have a mole on his back!

# CHAPTER SIX

GENEVRA fought back the sick, panicky feeling that clawed at the edges of her new-found happiness. Lots of people had moles removed, it meant nothing. The shape of his body, the way he made her feel...there could be no doubt that he was Luke, no matter what he called himself.

But she had been so sure the mole would be there. Its absence eroded her confidence, opening her mind to other disturbing thoughts. He had not confessed his deception, despite the most positive proof of her feelings towards him. He lay asleep in her arms as if he hadn't a care in the world. What if he really was Christian Nemo, a stranger whom she had only met yesterday?

No, that was impossible! Every instinct clamoured an instant rejection. He was no stranger!

And yet, when she had first met Luke, he hadn't felt like a stranger, either. Was it possible for two men to be so alike that she could love them both with the same intensity?

The idea tortured Genevra for several moments before it was forcefully dismissed. It was madness to even contemplate it after what had happened between them tonight. She knew him...knew him to the very depths of her being, and there had to be some way of proving that Luke and Christian were one and the same person.

She fretted over the problem until an answer slowly dawned. All she had to do was see his passport. Surely it would hold the truth. To adopt a false name in a foreign country where nobody knew you was a relatively simple matter, but she couldn't imagine it would be very simple to obtain a false passport.

The temptation to look for it became too great to resist. Very gently, she eased herself out of his embrace and slid silently off the bed. His trousers lay in a crumpled heap on the floor, and she picked them up and folded them neatly across the seat of a chair. She retrieved the coat which had been dropped near the doorway and, feeling uncomfortably like a sneak-thief, she checked the pockets.

The only contents was a slim leather wallet, and although it probably contained identifying credit cards Genevra could not bring herself to open it. She argued to herself that they wouldn't prove anything, anyway. A man who had gone to so much trouble in setting up this hotel project would almost certainly have covered his name-change on any cards he used. She had to find his passport.

It wasn't in his clothes, so it had to be in his room. She couldn't go there tonight, but at the first opportunity... the run of darting thoughts came to a dazed halt. Genevra stood in the middle of the room, appalled by what was happening to her. The man she loved had come back to her. Couldn't she show a little faith in him?

The physical barrier between them had been broken tonight, but there were other adjustments to be made... like with Johnny! Maybe he thought it was better to earn his son's love before presenting himself as his father. What other reason could he have for not declaring who he was? Maybe he would tell her first thing in the morning. All she really had to do was wait.

Her gaze shifted to the bed, and her eyes gloated lovingly over the powerfully muscled body that lay there. Her man, she thought with intense pride. There was something touchingly vulnerable about his nakedness that brought a lump of emotion to her throat. She suddenly remembered his uncertainty tonight when he had come to take her to dinner. He *was* vulnerable where she was concerned. She had to remember that, and not judge his words and actions too hastily.

He stirred in his sleep, his arm moving restlessly over the empty space where she had lain. Genevra ran back to the bed and snuggled up to him, lifting his arm around her waist. It instantly hugged her closer, and his mouth brushed against her temple.

'Genevra...' The dreamy sigh held so much longing and love that tears pricked her eyes.

'I'm here,' she whispered, her heart swelling with her love for him. 'I'll always be here.'

She awoke the next morning to find him looking down at her, a soft, wondering expression on his face. A satisfied little smile curved her lips. 'It wasn't a dream,' she assured him.

He laughed, and it was the sound of bubbling happiness. He said nothing about being an impostor, but somehow the omission didn't dim Genevra's pleasure at all as they made love, slowly and exquisitely. Then, wrapped in the thick, cosy bathrobes the hotel provided, they stole along the empty hallway to the Hydrangea Suite and made exhilarating use of the jacuzzi in his luxurious bathroom.

The bedroom was longer and narrower than Genevra's, but just as beautifully furnished. It had a balcony that overlooked the rose garden, and here they had breakfast brought to them. The sun was shining, the air was freshly scented and life was marvellous, far too marvellous to be entertaining any doubts whatsoever.

Even when she had the opportunity, Genevra didn't look for his passport. If Luke wanted to be Christian Nemo for a while, she didn't mind at all. As long as he was with her, loving her, a different name didn't mean a thing, and she even talked herself into calling him Christian.

They did not travel to St Ives in the Rolls-Royce. The car had been dismissed the previous afternoon. Christian had arranged for a helicopter to pick them up at the Manoir and fly them down. The countryside looked so pretty from the air that the whole trip was an absolute delight, but best of all was the aerial view of St Ives just before they landed.

The sea was sparkling, the beaches blazed white, colourfully dotted by the changing tents and deck-chairs and sunbathers and towels; the boats moored inside the harbour lent their picturesque flavour to the scene, and the neat nestling of the village around the waterfront tugged at Genevra's heart.

She had lived all her life here. She wondered how she would feel about leaving it when the time came.

She glanced at the man beside her. He smiled and squeezed her hand. The noise of the helicopter made conversation a shouting affair, but words were unnecessary between them at the moment. Genevra knew she would go anywhere with him...to Australia or America, or wherever his life was based now.

The helicopter landed on the front lawn of Tregenna Castle Hotel, which took up a dominant place on the hill above the village. The impressive façade, with its battlement-style walls and flags flying from the turrets that flanked the entrance, was largely accentuated by the extensive grounds which contained a private golf course, tennis courts, swimming pool, all edged with lovely trees and gardens. The hotel was a popular tourist place, and Genevra was not surprised when Christian had named it as their destination. It was where Luke had stayed during that long-ago summer.

He ordered a taxi as soon as they reached the reception desk, and declared his intention of seeing her safely home. Genevra smiled, sensing his eagerness to meet Johnny, and only too happy to comply with his wishes. He removed a large parcel from his luggage and grinned a little sheepishly at her as he laid it on top of her suitcase.

'A present for a little boy. I hope you don't mind. I thought ... well, I like kids, and I ...'

'I don't mind at all,' she said quickly, wanting him to have every possible joy in their son. Her own joy in his anticipation broke into a wide grin. 'What did you buy?'

He gave a dismissive shrug, trying to downplay any intensity of feeling. 'Oh, just a small race-track and a couple of remote-controlled cars. I'll help him set it up. If that's all right with you,' he added, unable to keep the hopeful appeal out of his voice.

'I'd be very grateful if you would,' she assured him. 'I'm not much good at mechanical things.'

The taxi arrived, and Christian wore a happy, satisfied smile all the way down to the waterfront where Genevra's shop was situated. He gave the taxi driver an enormous tip. Genevra was riding on a wild high as she led him into the bookshop.

Fortunately Beryl was attending to a customer, so Genevra did not have to stop and introduce him. She gave her assistant a 'hello' wave which was acknowledged with an interested lift of the eyebrows. Genevra grinned at her, mouthed 'later', then ushered Christian to the staircase at the back of the shop.

'I hope that race-track is small, because we haven't got much room up here,' she warned, ruefully recalling that the Hollyhock suite at the Manoir had been bigger than the floor above them. It was divided into four rooms: kitchen, living-room, bathroom, and Auntie May's bedroom, then the two attic bedrooms up another flight of stairs.

'It only needs about four feet of floor. I'll teach Johnny how to dismantle it,' Christian assured her.

And of course he knew where it would fit in the living-room, Genevra assured herself. Luke had been in her home dozens of times.

'I'm home!' she called, excitement spilling the words out as soon as she opened the door into the living-room.

'Mummy!' Johnny shrieked from the kitchen, and came pelting out to greet her.

Genevra swept him up into her arms, hugging him with a fierce mother-love as she turned to show him off to his father. And as Christian drank in the small, boyish features that stamped him as their son, Johnny stared back at him, his gray eyes widening with fascination.

'Are you a pirate?' he asked.

Christian laughed. 'I'm afraid not. But I did bring you some booty.'

He held out the parcel encouragingly, and Johnny wriggled down from Genevra's embrace to take possession of it. 'For me?' he asked, a little over-whelmed by the size of the gift.

'All for you,' Christian affirmed, his smile so en-gaging that Johnny instantly responded with a happy grin before excitement got the better of him and he bent his head over the intriguing parcel, giving it his full attention. Christian's hand reached out, instinctively wanting to touch, and in a loving, fatherly way it gently ruffled the dark, curly head that was so like his own.

Auntie May appeared in the kitchen doorway, obviously drawn by the strange voice. She looked Christian up and down as Genevra introduced them, her blue eyes alight with curiosity and her interest very definitely aroused when she realised that he was the publisher that Genevra had gone to meet in London.

She patted back the wisps of grey hair that had escaped the bun at the back of her head, straightened the cover-all apron she invariably wore in the kitchen, and almost twittered with pleasure at the honour of meeting him.

When Christian proceeded to explain his presence in St Ives, she fairly beamed with approval, her expression telling Genevra with every glance that this was a man who should be encouraged. In no time at all, she was pushing cups of tea and her home-made cookies at him, and she was so intent on making him feel welcome, she even insisted that he call her May, instead of Miss Kingsley.

Christian charmed her even further by getting down on the living-room floor to help Johnny set up the race-track and show him how to work the remote control for the cars. Johnny, of course, was beside himself with excitement at having such a marvellous toy to play with, and positively basked in the attention Christian gave him as they played races with the cars.

Genevra felt more intensely happy than she had ever done in her life. When she accompanied her aunt into the kitchen to cut some sandwiches for lunch, she couldn't help smiling broadly at Auntie May's sly observation that Christian would make a very good father.

'Doesn't he remind you of someone, Auntie May?' she asked impulsively.

A puzzled frown came and went. 'No, I can't say he does. Except...' The frown returned, accompanied by a firm shake of the head. 'It's time you forgot him, Genevra. Turn over a new leaf. Don't spoil anything by looking back.'

'But you felt it too, didn't you?' Genevra insisted, elated by the tacit admission.

'He has the same kind of confidence and charm. That's all.' She heaved a sigh. 'And you take care this time. Don't think I can't see what's in front of my eyes. You're as smitten with him as you were before.'

Genevra laughed and hugged her aunt in a rush of grateful affection. 'I promise I'll take care.'

Auntie May had come to live with Genevra and her father when George Kingsley had been struck down by his first heart attack eight years ago. She was his older sister, a spinster who had made a career of private nursing, and she had been kind and loving and supportive to Genevra from the very first day.

Genevra's mother had died young, and for a decade there had only been her father and herself, but Auntie May quickly took the place of a mother in Genevra's heart. Her aunt had seen her through the grief of her father's death and the grief of Luke's desertion, stood by her throughout her pregnancy, and helped to look after Johnny ever since he was born. How Genevra would have managed without her these last few years was too bleak a thought to even contemplate.

It was on the tip of her tongue to tell her aunt that Christian Nemo was, in fact, the same person she had met four years ago, but she bit down on the words, keeping them for a better time. He couldn't hold out on her much longer. Then he could tell Auntie May himself.

Despite the family atmosphere that prevailed, Christian said nothing that gave any hint of his true identity in front of Johnny or Auntie May. Genevra didn't really expect him to. But he certainly made an effective start of establishing himself in Johnny's affections before he took his leave of them after lunch.

'Would you be able to have dinner with me at the Castle tonight, Genevra?' he asked as she accompanied him downstairs.

'If you can wait until after I've put Johnny to bed. Eight o'clock?'

'Fine!'

And they smiled at each other, anticipation dancing in their eyes.

Tonight, Genevra thought with utter certainty. He would tell her tonight!

He came for her in a taxi, right on the dot of eight o'clock. Genevra was ready and waiting, and the moment he took her hand the excitement of last night started pumping through her. As they rode back up to the Castle, Christian spoke of Johnny, saying what a fine boy he was, and what a wonderful job she had done in turning him into such a bright, happy child. His comments gave her deep pleasure, but she could hardly think beyond the fact that they were together again.

'Every time I see you, you're even more beautiful,' Christian murmured as they walked into the hotel dining-room, and she knew he was feeling the same urgent desire.

As soon as they were seated at a table, the waiter handed them menus. Genevra's eyes ran through the courses listed, but the words didn't register on her fevered brain.

'What do you fancy?' Christian asked.

She looked at him. Her stomach curled at the way he looked at her.

'I'm not very hungry,' she said on a ragged breath.

'Neither am I,' he replied huskily. 'One course?'

She nodded.

They ordered roast beef.

The meal seemed to take for ever to come. They made small efforts to talk from time to time, but the words quickly trailed into silence again, swamped by the intensity of their desire for each other. They ate with single-minded purpose—to get the meal over. Then, with almost indecent haste, they left the dining-room.

'The elevator's slow,' Christian said.

They took the stairs.

Genevra suddenly laughed; a wild, slightly hysterical laugh. 'We're being quite mad,' she said.

'Yes,' Christian agreed. 'I'm not sure that I want to be sane ever again.'

A fierce wave of possessiveness made her ask, 'Have you ever felt like this with any other woman, Christian?'

'No.' He unlocked his door and swept her inside his room, hugging her tightly to him as he pushed the door shut. His mouth brushed across her temples with the same fervour that throbbed in his voice as he added, 'Only you, Genevra. Only you.'

And somehow that declaration lent an extra-special dimension to their lovemaking, giving Genevra the emotional security she had secretly craved. He was not only hers now, he had always been hers, despite his marriage and the years of separation. No other woman had ever stirred him so deeply.

Genevra thought she had known the ultimate contentment last night, but she had only brushed the surface of it. As she lay quietly in Christian's arms, after every passionate demand had been made and met, she felt that love had no limits. It could just go soaring on to infinity.

'Genevra?' His voice held a slightly tentative note that barely registered through the haze of her happiness.

'Yes?' she murmured, pressing her lips over his heart.

His fingers threaded through her hair to hold her head still, gently pressing for her full attention. She sensed the slight rise of tension in him even before he spoke again.

'There's something I want to tell you. And ask you. I hope...' His chest lifted as he drew in a quick breath. 'I hope you'll understand.'

She smiled, both relieved and elated that the moment of truth had come at last. 'I'm listening,' she said in soft encouragement.

'I have a daughter, Genevra...'

A daughter! All her happy anticipation withered into numb shock. He was the father of some other child besides Johnny...another woman's child! For him to have married another woman was painful enough, but to have fathered...and it was a daughter!

'She's a few months younger than Johnny,' he continued.

He said more. Genevra vaguely heard words floating over her head, but her mind was swamped with wave after wave of black jealousy. All this time he had been giving another child the love and attention that should have been Johnny's! A daughter... by the woman he had married... while his son... *their* son...

'Genevra?'

His tone implied he was waiting for an answer, but she hadn't heard the question. Her heart was still pounding in her ears. He moved, sliding down beside her so that he could make a more direct appeal. He tenderly pushed her tumbled hair away from her face, and even in the darkening shadows of twilight she could see his taut concern.

'To be like this with you . . . it's what I want most of all. But I can't ignore Felicity, Genevra, any more than you can ignore Johnny. They're parts of our lives. I want you to meet her. I want her to meet you and Johnny. I want . . .' He hesitated, then heaved a deep sigh. 'Is it too much to ask, or too soon to ask it?'

He was right, of course. Her rational mind told her so. She would never give up her son for anyone, and she couldn't expect him to put aside a daughter. Genevra fought back the jealousy, knowing that she had to accept the child if she wanted to have this man's love.

'Where is she?' Her voice sounded wary, reserved, and she made a more concentrated effort to meet his needs. 'I mean . . . I don't understand. Does she live with you?'

'Yes. And always has done. At present, Felicity is staying with her grandfather in London. She is happy with him, but it's only a temporary arrangement. I had intended flying back and forth to visit her but, now that I've met Johnny, I've been thinking . . . hoping . . . that our children might get on well together. But if I'm going too fast for you, Genevra, just tell me so.'

'No,' she answered quickly. The last thing she wanted was for him to back off from her. She would cope with his daughter somehow. 'When do you want me to meet her?'

He hesitated, but his eagerness was all too evident as he asked, 'Would tomorrow afternoon be too soon?'

Genevra swallowed hard and stuck to her resolution. 'I have to work in the shop tomorrow, Christian. But if you and your daughter would like to come for dinner at six o'clock tomorrow night, I'm sure that'll be fine.'

His relief and gratitude were poured into a long, tender kiss. 'Thank you,' he whispered huskily.

And for the first time Genevra felt she understood the conflict of interests that had driven him to adopt a different identity. Certainly there was the change in his physical appearance, but there were other changes in his life that had further-reaching consequences . . . like his daughter! And, despite her love for him, Genevra knew that accepting the child of his marriage was not going to be easy.

# CHAPTER SEVEN

GENEVRA was miserable. Auntie May thought it lovely that Christian Nemo had a little girl of Johnny's age, and Johnny was all excited about the 'family' dinner-party.

The two of them had been happily planning the menu for tonight when Genevra left to open the bookshop. Ashamed of her own lack of enthusiasm, she had been glad of the excuse to remove herself from any more talk of Felicity.

She tried to reason herself out of the reserve she felt. Whatever the sins of the parents, a child could not be held accountable for them. Felicity was even younger than Johnny, a total innocent, deserving of being accepted for herself. Genevra recited all this over and over again, yet still the jealousy nibbled at her, and it wasn't entirely on Johnny's account, either.

If Felicity favoured her mother in looks instead of her father, Genevra didn't know how she was going to bear it. To have a living reminder of the woman he had married, right under her eyes all the time...just the thought of such an eventuality made her feel sick.

It took hours of intense resolution to fight the black feeling into a neutral grey. That marriage was finished. Nothing could be gained by brooding over the past, and a happy future depended on her accepting Felicity, whatever she was like.

The day sped by all too fast, and Christian arrived ten minutes early. He walked into the shop while Genevra was still serving a customer, and her heart sank at first sight of the little girl at his side. She was beautiful—too beautiful for Genevra's peace of mind—and her features bore no relationship to Johnny whatsoever.

Father and daughter stood by one of the bookstands, waiting for her to be free for them, and Genevra was extremely conscious of two big brown eyes peering up at her from under a wheat-gold fringe. The shiny fair hair fell to just below her shoulders, straight and thickly textured enough to look good at that length. She wore a dainty but not overly fussy dress in a blue and white Laura Ashley print. Long white socks showed off sweetly curved legs, and her feet were encased in pretty blue shoes. She leaned shyly against her father's leg and chewed on her lower lip, obviously apprehensive about meeting strangers.

Genevra ushered the customer out of the shop, quickly locked the door after him, then fixed a determined smile on her face before turning to greet her two visitors. Christian smiled back at her, but the little girl's face remained grave.

The brown eyes seemed to grow more enormous as Genevra crouched down in front of her, and the hopeful appeal in them was so touching that Genevra could not resist it. Her smile warmed into real welcome. 'Hello,' she said softly.

'Hello.' It was a shy little echo. Felicity drew a quick breath and thrust out the small, gift-wrapped packet she had been holding. 'Daddy and me bought this for you.'

'How kind! Thank you both very much. May I open it now?'

Felicity gravely nodded. Genevra wondered if she ever smiled, and wished she'd had the foresight to buy her a gift. Too late now, she thought regretfully, and quickly unwrapped what turned out to be a velvet jeweller's box. Her pulse leapt erratically as she opened the lid. On a bed of white satin lay an exquisite Victorian necklace, a delicate pattern of gold suspending a beautiful, heart-shaped amethyst.

'Daddy said your eyes were that colour,' Felicity said in a breathy little rush.

'Do you think so?' Genevra asked.

Another grave nod.

'It's the loveliest gift I've ever been given. Would you hold the box for me while I put the necklace on?'

Felicity took the box and stared fixedly at Genevra as she fastened the catch and centered the pendant at the base of her throat. 'Have I got it right?'

Again came the nod. Then she looked up at her father for his approval. Christian smiled down at her, prompting her into offering a shy little smile to Genevra.

'I have a little boy who's been looking forward to meeting you all day,' Genevra said encouragingly. 'In fact, he got Auntie May to cook a chocolate cake, just because you were coming. Do you like chocolate cake?'

Another nod.

'Then let's go upstairs.' Genevra held out her hand as she straightened up, and a little hand crept into it. Genevra had the feeling that she had just won a marathon, and the grateful look that Christian gave her made every step of it worth while.

Johnny virtually pounced on Felicity the moment they appeared in the living-room, and the little girl tamely followed in his ebullient wake as he showed her everything that he considered of interest to a kindred spirit. Johnny simply didn't recognise shyness, and he soon coaxed his very obliging new playmate on to the living-room floor, where he quickly demonstrated how to operate one of the remote-controlled cars. Felicity concentrated hard on pleasing Johnny, and he absolutely adored being looked to as the authority on everything.

Auntie May quickly winkled Felicity out of her shyness when they sat down to dinner. The little girl chattered away to her as if she had known her all her life, but, where Genevra was concerned, she remained tongue-tied. The big brown eyes kept stealing glances at her but, whenever Genevra tried to engage the child in conversation, Felicity instantly reverted to nods, almost as if she was afraid to speak to her in case she said something wrong.

It was highly disconcerting, particularly since Genevra now wanted to win the little girl's affection. She was intensely grateful when dinner was over, and Auntie May tactfully shepherded the children into the living-room to play, leaving Genevra and Christian alone to do the dishes.

'Why is Felicity so shy with me?' she asked him anxiously. 'Am I doing something wrong?'

'No, not a thing,' he assured her.

'But . . .'

He pulled her into his arms and pressed her close to him, rubbing his cheek over her hair. 'I told Felicity that you're a very special person, and that you're important to me. Perhaps she's a little afraid of what that might mean to her.'

He drew back a little, and his expression held a plea for understanding. 'Felicity has had a lot of upsets in her short life, Genevra. They were unavoidable, but they've left her with certain fears that are difficult to counteract. She's not old enough to reason very well. She needs time to come to terms with what's taking place. That's all.'

Any last trace of jealousy was wiped out by Christian's explanation of his daughter's behaviour. Genevra felt a strong wave of compassion for the little girl. Johnny had never had a moment's doubt of his place in Genevra's and Auntie May's life. He had been wrapped in a secure cocoon of love from the moment he was born. The years that followed had an unbroken pattern which imbued him with a natural confidence that had never even been shaken.

'I'm afraid Johnny doesn't know the meaning of fear,' Genevra remarked with a dry smile.

'Neither do you,' Christian murmured huskily. 'I've never seen anyone give their trust so readily. You've done so much for me, I'll be for ever in your debt, Genevra.'

'It's enough that you're here with me,' she whispered, and kissed him with all the fierce conviction of the love that had been waiting years for such whole-hearted expression.

In the days that followed, Christian had many opportunities to confess the truth of the past to Genevra, but he turned aside all her attempts to lead him into it. He embraced the present as if there was no past . . . or none that he had any inclination to recall. And gradually Genevra thought less and less about it, too happy with their relationship to drag it into question.

Christian took the children out every day. They built sandcastles on the beach, flew kites at Land's End, went out on a fishing-boat, visited the ruins of King Arthur's castle at Tintagel . . . always some exciting or interesting activity that brought them home with glowing faces and shining eyes.

Auntie May frequently accompanied them, and Genevra too, whenever Beryl was available to take over the shop. From the very first day, Johnny adopted a big-brother attitude to Felicity, encouraging her to follow wherever he led, and quickly dismissing any nervous reluctance on her part by showing what fun everything was. The little girl blossomed into a happy, carefree child under Johnny's tutelage, and slowly but surely her shyness with Genevra was overcome.

One week slipped into another. No mention was made of visiting another hotel for the book project. In fact, Genevra hadn't written a word on Le Manoir Aux Quat'Saisons, and Christian hadn't asked for it. Their involvement with each other was so deep and immediate that nothing else mattered. Whenever Genevra thought of the book proposition she smiled to herself, sure in her own mind that it had only ever been a means to the end which had already been achieved.

The inquiry that she had asked Matthew Hastings to carry out on Luke Stanford had also lost any relevance to her. It had actually slipped so far out of her mind that she did not initially connect it with Matthew's startling appearance in her bookshop on the Saturday afternoon, just over two weeks after her visit to him.

'Matthew! What brings you all the way to St Ives?' she exclaimed, surprised to see him away from his London habitat.

He cast a troubled frown at a browsing customer. 'When will you be free, Genevra? I'd like to see you alone. Somewhere private, if that's possible.'

The request brought a nervous flutter to Genevra's heart. The gravity of Matthew's manner suggested that it was important, yet she couldn't imagine why he had felt it necessary to make a personal visit on her behalf. That this wealthy old London bachelor would spend a whole day of his free time on coming to see her seemed incredible.

Then she remembered the inquiry. If Matthew had found out that Luke Stanford was in England, he might feel distressed for her. Matthew had always treated her in a fatherly way, taking a kindly and sincere interest in her personal welfare. It would genuinely upset him to see her hurt and, if he could do anything to prevent it, he would.

Feeling reassured about Matthew's purpose for this visit, Genevra quickly eased the customer out of the shop and locked up. She invited Matthew to follow her upstairs, thinking that it would be curiously ironic if Christian came back with Auntie May and the children while the solicitor was still presenting his evidence.

She saw Matthew settled in the most comfortable armchair in the living-room, propped herself on the armrest of another, and smiled her appreciation of his kind consideration. 'You shouldn't have done it, Matthew, but it's terribly good of you to come all this way for me.'

'I had nothing else to do,' he said in casual dismissal, as his shrewd blue eyes observed her keenly. 'You look more relaxed and happy than when I saw you last, Genevra.'

She laughed. 'I have reason to be. Life couldn't be better at the moment.'

'I'm relieved to hear it.' He nodded a couple of times, then remarked rather heavily, 'Much better to live in the present than dwell on the past. I was concerned that the news I have for you . . . I wasn't sure how you'd react.'

'Not badly now, Matthew,' she assured him, confident that she knew what was on his mind. 'It's about Luke Stanford, isn't it?'

'Yes. You wanted to know if he was still married...'

'And he's not,' Genevra rushed on.

'That's true,' Matthew nodded gravely. 'The marriage ended three years ago. When his wife died.'

'She...died?' Genevra echoed, more in shock than disbelief. She hadn't actually asked Christian what had happened with his wife, more or less taking it for granted that they had been through a rather nasty divorce, since Felicity was in his custody.

'From some kind of kidney failure related to acute nephritis,' Matthew said in confirmation.

Genevra felt discomfited by this knowledge. She had certainly wanted the marriage dissolved, but not through death. Death didn't give anyone a choice.

Matthew rose from his chair and came over to her, taking her hand and putting his other arm around her shoulders in a comforting hug. 'It's never pleasant to hear about another's death,' he said in soft sympathy.

She flashed him an ironic look. 'I didn't know her. Not even her name. But I wasn't expecting that.'

'No. One never does with young people.' He sighed and looked even more troubled. 'I'm sorry, Genevra...' He paused, biting his lower lip, then dragging in another breath before he continued, 'Luke Stanford only survived his wife by a few weeks...'

The quiet statement sent a queer little chill through Genevra's heart. She looked sharply at Matthew, unable to accept his choice of words. 'That can't be right! Luke is alive. I know it!' she rapped out impatiently.

'He's dead, Genevra. He's been dead for the last three years.'

'No!' She could feel the blood draining from her face even as she pushed herself up from the chair to vehemently deny what Matthew was saying. 'I don't believe it! It can't be so!'

But there was no evasion in Matthew's eyes. They were soft with compassion, but steadily intent on making her face irrefutable facts. 'He was a passenger in a light plane which crashed just after take-off, killing everyone on board. There's no question about it, Genevra. The inquiry agent sent a photocopy of a newspaper report on the crash. The plane exploded into flames soon after impact with the ground. There were no survivors.'

Her hand lifted to her forehead, but she couldn't still the sickening whirl in her mind...

Dead...

Luke was dead...

Dead . . .

She felt herself falling, but the blackness was rushing in on her, and she couldn't push it back. For the first time in her life, Genevra fainted.

## CHAPTER EIGHT

'GENEVRA! Genevra!'

Someone was calling her name, patting her hand, stroking her face, drawing her out of the black, dizzying well that had swallowed her. She struggled to meet the urgency in the voice, wanting to answer it. She forced her eyes open, and Matthew Hastings' face swam in front of her. Memory came flooding back, and a moan of sheer anguish tore from her throat.

'I'm most terribly sorry, my dear. I thought it would be a shock, but . . . stupid of me not to lead into it more gradually. All my fault . . .'

The agitated bursts of speech served as a goad for Genevra to gather some control over herself. She was in an armchair. Matthew was fussing over her. Luke was dead. He had not come back to her. He never would. And Christian Nemo was . . . Christian Nemo.

Somehow, she managed a wan smile to appease Matthew's concern. 'I've never fainted before. Thanks for looking after me, Matthew. I'll be fine now.'

He was not completely convinced, eyeing her pale listlessness with a worried frown. 'I'll make you a cup of tea. Best thing. You just sit there, Genevra. I'll manage.'

She didn't protest, although she vaguely wondered if Matthew had ever made a pot of tea in his life before. A man of his position and wealth would have always had it served to him, but she heard him clattering around in the kitchen and supposed he knew what he was doing. It didn't really matter, anyway. She needed the time to straighten things out in her mind.

She found it almost impossible to accept that Christian wasn't Luke. Her emotions were so entwined with that identification that she was frightened to even try to separate them. How much of her love belonged to Luke, how much to Christian? She had established her present love on the past. Take that foundation away, and what did she have left?

How could her instincts have been so wrong?

And why hadn't she felt something . . . a sense of loss . . . something . . . when Luke's life had ended?

Three years . . . three years of waiting and hoping and still loving him, and all that time he had been dead! It didn't feel right. Yet how could she deny it? Matthew certainly wouldn't lie to her, and the inquiry agent had no reason to report anything but the truth.

But Christian was the living proof that . . . Genevra shook her head, forcing herself to acknowledge that there was no proof. Christian had denied being Luke. There had been no mole on his back. He had never given her any real evidence that he was Luke. She had simply interpreted his actions and responses in ways that supported her own secret belief, and turned a wilfully blind eye to anything that didn't.

All along she had been emotionally committed to a man who didn't exist any more. Dead... killed... his life wasted for no purpose or reason. Just another victim of a plane crash.

Tears welled into Genevra's eyes and trickled down her cheeks as that long-ago summer of happiness rolled through her mind, bringing back the memory of Luke's intense vitality, the warmth and strength of him. Was such a futile death a fitting climax of all that passion for life?

Grief swelled from Genevra's heart. Luke had loved her. She had never doubted that, not even when the letter came. And they'd had so little time together. She wished she had written to him, telling him about Johnny. He should have known he had a son. It might have been some consolation to him in those last few moments when he must have known death was inevitable. Had he thought of her? Why hadn't she felt something? How could he be alive to her all these years when he was dead?

Matthew returned with a tea-tray, which he set down on the small table near her chair. He pulled his own chair closer and kept a sympathetic silence until Genevra had mopped up her tears. He poured out the tea, adding the appropriate amounts of milk and sugar. Practically every time she had visited his office, Matthew had fixed her appointment around morning or afternoon tea. She suddenly realised he had never really treated her in a businesslike fashion.

'You've always been so kind to me,' she blurted out. 'Why is that, Matthew?'

A soft, whimsical smile curled his mouth. 'In my line of business, you mostly see the worst side of human nature—greed, envy, hatred, malice. But you, Genevra, have shown me over and over again that there is another side. You needed so much and asked for so little. I've always found it a rare pleasure to be with you, and talk with you.'

He heaved a sigh and gave a sad shake of his head. 'If I could give you happiness, I would, but not even wealth can manufacture happiness.' His eyes met hers with a sudden gleam of sharp determination. 'But what I can do is save you some grief over Luke Stanford.'

Tears pricked her eyes again, and she had to swallow hard to get rid of the lump in her throat. She was deeply touched by what Matthew had said of his feeling for her, but he didn't understand about Luke. 'I know it looks bad . . . that he left me as he did, but Luke did love me, Matthew.'

'No!' His mouth thinned with barely repressed anger. 'He never did! I'm sorry, Genevra, he sold you out. He married money, a great deal of it, and gave you away. And that's what I want you to face. Luke Stanford wasn't worthy of your love, and the sooner you realise that, the sooner you can dismiss him from your heart.'

She stared at him disbelievingly, her eyes still sheened with tears. 'You don't know what you're saying, Matthew. You didn't know him.'

'Did *you* really know him, Genevra?' he asked in a gentler tone. 'Just listen to the facts and judge for yourself. To begin with, the woman he married was virtually his sister...'

Protest burst from her lips. 'That's not possible! It can't be so!' It was illegal, unnatural, and the man she had known was good and fine and...

'Victoria Preston was no blood-relation, but she was his sister in every other sense,' Matthew cut back with prosecuting force. 'Luke Stanford was the foster son of John Preston. He'd lived in the Preston household since childhood. When he married Preston's daughter, and only child, Victoria, he married into a full half-share of Preston's construction company. And that partnership was worth at least twelve million dollars, probably more.'

Genevra's mind was reeling with the implications that Matthew was forcing on her, but still she clutched to her faith in Luke's basic honesty. 'There were family problems. He had to help them. That's why...'

'Open your eyes, Genevra!' Matthew retorted, then continued with implacable logic. 'The partnership was tied to the marriage. The Preston construction company was a success story. Luke Stanford chose the security of wealth and position. The price he had to pay was letting you go. And he did! You see, my dear, when it comes to that much money, love invariably comes second. And you were a long way away.'

Matthew's face was drawn into lines of weary cynicism as he added, 'It happens often enough, Genevra. I've seen it many times. A chance at the jackpot comes along, and love flies out the window. When you have wealth, you can have your choice of any number of women. Whatever he said to you in excuse for his betrayal was only window-dressing. The cold, hard truth is...you were dispensable.'

He hitched himself forwards in his chair in earnest appeal. 'Don't waste any more time or emotion on Luke Stanford, Genevra. He's dead. Bury him, and get on with your own life.'

Every word of Matthew's relentless exposition had left her feeling a little more hollow and uncertain. Had she been fooling herself all these years, living on a fantasy of her making? Like the fantasy she had built around Christian? She didn't know what was true any more, couldn't trust her own judgements.

She sat in a numb daze, so shaken and confused that there didn't seem to be anything she could hold fast to. Luke was a shattered image. Christian had been coloured with figments of her imagination. Her eyes lifted helplessly to Matthew's, recognising him as the one dependable solid in a sea of shifting uncertainties.

'What will I do?' she whispered.

'Stop looking back,' Matthew answered promptly. 'Think about expanding your horizons. Do some travelling. Use the trust money, Genevra. Invest in your own life. You're in a static rut here.' He raised his eyebrows in quizzical fashion. 'Did anything come of that meeting you had with the publisher in London?'

Colour flooded back into Genevra's face. Far too much had eventuated from that first meeting with Christian, and yet . . . could she honestly say she regretted any of it? 'Yes. Yes it did,' she said slowly.

'So what are you writing about now?'

Her smile twisted with irony. 'Nothing really. It's more a personal thing. Christian brought me back to St Ives. He's staying up at Tregenna Castle.'

'Ah!' said Matthew, with such a satisfied air that Genevra's cheeks burnt even more fiercely. 'He's . . . uh . . . not married, is he, Genevra?'

'He was. But not any more,' she muttered, thinking how stupid she was not to have questioned Christian with more persistence. In actual fact, she knew very little about him, just as she had known very little about Luke. Matthew was so right. It was well past time she opened her eyes, instead of acting on blind instinct.

'Well, if he's in the publishing business, no doubt you have much in common,' Matthew declared cheerfully.

It suddenly struck Genevra that she and Christian had barely spoken of books since that afternoon at Le Manoir Aux Quat'Saisons. She really knew nothing about his business, beyond what he had told her at the Dorchester. She hadn't even believed in it then.

'We do have children in common,' she said, seizing on the one definite parallel in their lives. 'Christian has a little girl a few months younger than Johnny. He and Auntie May have taken them both down to the beach this afternoon.'

'Splendid!' said Matthew with ringing approval. 'Does Johnny like him?'

'Yes.'

Even though Christian wasn't Johnny's real father, and Felicity wasn't Johnny's half-sister, the sense of a family unit had developed over the last two weeks. That was real enough, and Genevra grasped on to it as if it was a lifeline into the future.

Christian Nemo was a good man, a caring parent, and a wonderful lover. Even though he wasn't Luke, he wasn't any less than the man she thought he had been. Possibly, he was more!

Matthew suddenly grinned. 'So that was why you had a shopping spree at Harrods! And why you looked happy when I arrived. I hope this Christian—what's his full name, Genevra?'

'Nemo. Christian Nemo.'

'Nemo,' Matthew echoed musingly. 'What a curious name!'

'He's an American,' Genevra supplied helpfully, recalling now that he had never once sounded the least bit Australian.

Matthew shook his head. 'Nemo is Latin, Genevra. In English, it means no one. Still, with Americans, anything is possible.' He smiled benevolently at her. 'And how do you find his daughter? A likeable child?'

'Yes. She's very sweet.' And all her heartburn over Felicity had been based on a totally false premise, Genevra thought ruefully. She had no more reason to be jealous of Felicity's existence than Christian had to be jealous of Johnny's.

'Well then, I'm glad I came down and got this Luke Stanford business cleared away.' Matthew stood up with an air of beaming optimism. 'As I said, nothing to be gained by dwelling on the past. I'll be going now, Genevra.'

She rose from the chair and Matthew took her hands in his, giving them a light squeeze. 'You have my best wishes, my dear.'

'Thank you.' She leaned forwards and pressed a grateful kiss on his cheek.

Matthew's eyes twinkled with pleasure. 'And don't be worrying about the Anna Christie Trust, either. I'll let you know all about it when the report comes in.'

'It's not urgent, Matthew. Just curiosity, really. But I do appreciate, very deeply, all you've done on my behalf.'

His mouth quirked. 'I must admit that this little trip wasn't exactly for your sake, Genevra. It has lifted a burden from my mind. Now I can look forward to seeing you next time.'

Genevra escorted him downstairs and saw him on his way. She did not reopen the shop for business. There was little enough time left before she would have to face Christian again, and she was afraid that she would no longer react naturally to him.

The cold, hard facts stated that Luke Stanford had been dead for three years. Barely two hours ago, Genevra had thought she was waving him off to the beach with Auntie May and the children. But the man who would return...who was he? What did he really mean to her?

She thought she had known Luke through and through, yet he had proved to be faithless and mercenary. Matthew had to be right. Luke hadn't really loved her, or he wouldn't have sacrificed the future they could have shared, no matter how much money he had been offered. An engineer with his years of experience could have earned a good living anywhere. They wouldn't have been penniless. Life might not have been so easy, but at least they would have had each other.

How could he have put her aside so soon after... had his loving her all been a lie? Had she only ever been a holiday affair to him, a bit of magical fantasy that had worn off as soon as he had returned to the reality of his life in Australia?

Genevra shook her head in hurt bewilderment as the words of his letter drifted once more through her mind. All a lie, she thought with a deep sense of desolation, a romantic lie to end a romantic interlude that had had no lasting meaning for him. The only genuine sentiment he had written was the last line: 'It will be best for both of us to try and forget what could have been.' And no doubt so many millions of dollars were a great aid to forgetting!

Bitterness welled over the hurt, and Genevra curled herself into an armchair and opened the door on her memories of Luke Stanford, reviewing them all with a new-born cynicism.

She had been a naïve, trusting fool, handing him her heart on a platter, believing all his empty promises. Luke Stanford had used her, used her and dropped her when she no longer meant anything to him.

Bury him, Matthew had advised, and the weight of Genevra's disillusionment buried him deep.

So intense was her brooding over the past, she didn't at first hear the noises that heralded the return of the children with Auntie May and Christian Nemo. It was the sound of footsteps on the stairs that first impinged upon her consciousness and, as Genevra realised what that sound meant, a rush of curdling panic shot her out of the chair.

She wanted to run away and hide, do anything that would keep Christian at a distance until she could adjust herself to this new situation. But there was no escape from what she had done and, even as she teetered on the point of flight, the living-room door was pushed open.

# CHAPTER NINE

THE children gave Genevra a few moments to gather a semblance of normal composure before facing the man to whom she had so recklessly and wantonly given her love.

Johnny burst into the living-room with Felicity at his heels, their faces aglow with excitement, and Genevra focused her attention on them, desperate for any distraction that postponed the inevitable confrontation.

'Felicity's staying here with me tonight,' Johnny crowed. 'Auntie May's going to fix a bed for her in my room so we can talk and talk and talk.'

'Yes!' Felicity breathed, her big brown eyes sparkling with delight.

Brown eyes, and Christian's a tawny-brown . . . God, what a fool she had been! Genevra forced a smile. 'Aren't you going to sleep at all?'

'If Felicity gets tired, I'll let her go to sleep,' Johnny granted handsomely, then grabbed Felicity's hand. 'Come on. There's cookies in the kitchen.'

'You children wash your hands first,' Auntie May called as they skipped off.

'Yes, Auntie May,' they chorused.

She slanted a knowing look at Genevra in passing. 'And don't be worrying about them tonight. They'll be just fine with me.' She looked back before following the children into the kitchen, a sly twinkle enlivening her eyes. 'And I'm sure Christian will look after you.'

Genevra's heart lurched at the meaningful emphasis her aunt gave the words. It implied a further development to the relationship which was already far too intimate for Genevra's peace of mind. Every nerve in her body quivered with apprehension when Christian's arm curled around her shoulders, turning her into a loose embrace. She hoped that none of her fears showed as she reluctantly met his smiling gaze.

'I'm taking you somewhere special tonight,' he said in a voice that throbbed with suppressed excitement. 'Will you wear that beautiful pink dress for me, Genevra? And pack an overnight bag.'

'An overnight...' Genevra bit her lips as panic surged again.

He chuckled, misreading the burning rush of colour to her cheeks. 'We're not going to offend your aunt's sensibilities. May approves of my intentions.' He dropped a teasing kiss on her forehead. 'I'll be back for you in an hour.'

Genevra stood rooted to the spot for several moments after Christian had left. Her blood ran hot and cold as she contemplated the kind of night

Christian had in mind. He was going to propose marriage to her! How else would he get Auntie May's approval of his intentions? And he had every right to expect Genevra to welcome his proposal and be madly happy about spending a night of love with him. And she would have been...up until a few hours ago!

What had she done? And what could she do now? Impossible to explain to him that she had thought he was someone else. It would be so insulting. She couldn't hurt Christian like that. He loved her. And she had wilfully and wantonly encouraged his love, even to the point of seducing him when he would have held back to give their relationship time to grow. She had made her bed with a vengeance, and now...did she have any other choice but to lie in it?

In a daze of frightening indecision, Genevra forced herself to get moving. Christian expected her to be ready for him at six-thirty. Auntie May expected it. The children expected it. She was trapped in a web of her own making, and there was no backing out of the situation. She had to face up to Christian and...and what? Accept him, or make some hopelessly contrived excuse for putting him off?

With a sickening dread in her heart, she bathed and dressed and packed an overnight bag. Her nakedness in the bath reminded her too sharply of

Christian's intimate knowledge of her body. She put on a bra under her pink dress, ashamed of the way she had flaunted herself on that first night. And, as she packed the bag, she was all too aware that Christian would not have arranged a separate room for her tonight.

She heard him arrive. The children shrilled happy greetings. Auntie May called out for her. Genevra took a deep breath, picked up her bag, and slowly descended the stairs from her attic bedroom. Her legs felt wobbly and unreliable. Her heart was a painful hammer. Her mouth was an arid desert.

Christian had both children juggled in his arms, and all three faces turned towards Genevra, their eyes shining happily at her. She paused on the stairs, her pulse beating even faster as she felt the emotional tug of the man and the boy and the girl, linked together in a powerful claim on her heart.

'You look so pretty, Mummy!' Johnny said proudly.

'Beautiful!' Felicity declared in round-eyed admiration.

Christian smiled.

Genevra's gaze fastened on the smile, and she tried her utmost to separate it from her memory of Luke.

Christian put the children down and moved forwards to take the bag from her hand. He was dressed in the dark grey suit he had worn at the

Dorchester, and he was an impressive figure of a man, so very masculine. The black patch over his eye gave him a rakish air that was both intriguing and sexy.

His smile tilted in amusement. 'You look as if you were seeing me for the first time.'

The awful irony of these words was not lost on Genevra. 'I was just thinking how handsome you are,' she said, hoping that she didn't sound as strained as she felt.

He laughed and took her hand to draw her down the last two stairs. 'I've got a taxi waiting for us.'

Genevra felt dreadfully self-conscious as she kissed the children goodbye and took her leave of Auntie May. Christian took her arm in a proprietorial way, making her tremblingly aware of how many times he had possessed her. Physically! There was no doubting that she still found him immensely attractive, but her mind and emotions were in terrible chaos.

He sat close to her in the taxi, his fingers threaded through hers, stroking across the back of her hand. Genevra felt choked by the sheer magnetism of his presence. She wished that Matthew had never come, that she had never been told that the man beside her could not be Luke. But that emotional security had been ripped away from her, and she couldn't pretend otherwise.

'Where are you taking me?' she asked as the taxi headed out of town.

Again he smiled, making her heart lurch with the happy look of anticipation that lit his face. 'To Boscundle Manor. It's near St Austell, and I've booked us in for the night.'

Another exclusive country hotel, Genevra thought with a guilty pang. 'Christian, I didn't write an article about Le Manoir Aux Quat'Saisons,' she confessed.

'Genevra, this has nothing to do with the project we discussed. It's only to do with you and me, and planning for the future.'

The future together, he meant, and Genevra still had no answer to the proposal which intuition told her was hovering on his lips. The need for evasion, postponement, made her grasp for some other line of conversation, and she chattered on about the children, asking Christian what they had done this afternoon.

He obliged her with an amusing description of the children's activities, and out of the turmoil in Genevra's mind came one absolute certainty— Johnny would benefit from having Christian as his stepfather. Christian really did like children. And she herself was very drawn to his shy little daughter. If she accepted Christian as a husband...

And why not? a savage little voice urged. Luke Stanford had married for the security of wealth.

She wouldn't ever have to worry about money again if she married Christian. Why shouldn't she be just as mercenary as the man who had betrayed her? What was love worth, anyway? A lot of heartache and bitter disillusionment!

It wasn't as if she didn't like Christian. And she could hardly say she shrank from sharing his bed! On any common-sense level she would be a fool to reject the future he could offer her. Luke was dead. He had never even been the man she had clung on to in her dreams, anyway. It was Christian who had unwittingly fulfilled her fantasy, being the kind of man she had thought Luke was. Maybe she *did* love Christian. At least he was real, she thought fiercely.

Boscundle Manor was a lovely old building, partially Georgian in style, but with many rambling additions that gave it a charming informality. Its beautiful hillside garden and the adjoining woodland gave the whole setting a peaceful, rural atmosphere. Genevra's inner tension eased a little as she stepped out of the taxi. There was a sense of solid permanence about the place that was vaguely comforting.

Genevra felt bone-weary of uncertainties. She looked up at Christian, who wanted to offer her something solid and permanent, and she made her decision. She wanted what he could give her, and in return she would be a good wife to him, and a good mother to Felicity.

They were greeted by a very welcoming couple and shown to their room, which was furnished with an elegant simplicity that was also comforting. Genevra did not want to be distracted from the decision which needed all her concentration if she wasn't to waver again. As soon as she and Christian were left alone, he drew her into his arms and she pressed closer, needing the physical reassurance of his warmth and strength.

'Hold me tight, Christian,' she whispered urgently. 'Never let me go.'

'Never!' he vowed with a deep conviction that was emphasised by the aggressive power of his body as he wrapped her in a crushing embrace. 'Say you'll marry me, Genevra. I can't wait any longer. It has to be. It has to be,' he repeated with such a yearning ache in his voice that Genevra's heart instinctively surrendered to it without any urging from her mind.

'I'll marry you, Christian,' she answered, and felt a tidal wave of relief, as if all responsibility for her actions had been lifted from her shoulders.

And she felt relief wash through him, too—the ragged expulsion of breath, the light shudder that ran through his body. He pressed a fervent trail of kisses over her hair, interspersing them with murmurs of love that floated into her mind and kept all doubts at bay.

He loosened his embrace to smile down at her; a funny little smile, mixed with apology and self-mockery. 'I've done this all wrong. I meant to make it a big moment with champagne and . . .' He sighed and dragged a small velvet pouch from his pocket. His fingers shook a little as he fumbled it open and withdrew a ring—a fabulous, deep blue sapphire, surrounded by diamonds.

'I hope it fits,' he breathed as he took her left hand and slid the ring on to her third finger.

'It's beautiful, Christian,' Genevra whispered, awed by the glittering size of the stones.

The ring faltered on her second knuckle, with Christian loath to give it the necessary push, but Genevra quickly thrust it into place.

'It fits,' she smiled up at him.

He laughed out of sheer exuberant feeling. 'I'll be even happier to see a wedding ring with it. I can't tell you how much this means to me, Genevra. I feel as if . . .' He shook his head, and once more took her in his arms and held her close, his cheek rubbing softly over her hair. 'It's as if I've waited all my life for this moment.'

Genevra was intensely moved by the wistful note of longing in that soft murmur. She didn't even think of herself. She just wanted to fulfil his dreams and make him happy.

He took her down to a dining-room, which gleamed with polished mahogany and shining silverware, but the glow of happiness on Christian's face outshone everything else. They drank champagne. They feasted on sole Véronique, and duckling with cherry and brandy sauce. They talked of the future.

'Where will we live?' Genevra asked.

'Wherever you wish,' Christian replied with grand unconcern.

'But what about your business?' she queried.

'I employ people who are paid a great deal, more than they are worth, to make sure that all my business interests keep running smoothly and successfully. I don't need to work, Genevra, and neither do you. You will never have to worry about money again,' he said with almost grim satisfaction.

'But . . . I have to consider Auntie May,' she protested worriedly.

'May is only too happy to come and live with us, wherever we go. She fancies the role of nanny to our children.'

'You've already spoken to her?'

'This afternoon.'

Genevra shook her head in bemusement. 'You've really thought of everything, haven't you?'

'Everything I can that will make you happy to be my wife,' he said with an intensity of feeling that humbled Genevra.

'I hope I can be everything you want in a wife, Christian,' she said with deep sincerity.

He looked at her with so much love and desire that her toes curled. 'You *are* everything, Genevra. Everything I've ever dreamed of and wanted and needed. If I couldn't have you, I wouldn't want to live.'

'Don't say that,' she implored, a little frightened that his happiness depended so much on her.

'It's true.' A faintly self-mocking smile curved his lips as he saw her reluctance to believe him. 'When we met at the Dorchester...I felt it then. I knew I had to do all I could to keep you in my life.'

And suddenly Genevra remembered her own strong reaction to him, the sensation that somehow their lives were inexorably intertwined...and that had been *before* she reasoned out that Christian and Luke were one and the same person. She had actually felt that she shouldn't walk away from Christian Nemo, which was why she had agreed to a test run of the project he had outlined.

She stared at him, her heart pounding with wild excitement over the revelation. It was Christian himself who had drawn that response from her, not a superimposed image of Luke Stanford! Christian, the man she was going to marry, joining her life with his for the rest of her days. Her instincts had not been wrong at all. This was a man she could love, *did* love!

'Yes,' she murmured, awed by the certainty that thrilled through her.

His hand reached across the table and gripped hers. 'You felt it, too?' he asked, emotion furring his voice.

She nodded. 'I hated it when you made that comment about Beauty and the Beast. I wanted to take away all the hurts you had suffered and make you...' She hesitated, groping for the right words to express her feelings.

'...and make me whole,' Christian supplied softly. 'You did that, Genevra. And I'll spend the rest of my life loving you in every way I can, because you make life worth while.'

He meant it. He really did need her. She was necessary to him. Genevra was swept by the most extraordinary feeling, as if the whole purpose of her existence had lain dormant until this moment. She had thought her life had no meaning, but it did. Christian gave it meaning. And purpose.

'Thank you,' she breathed, her whole body pulsing with a glorious exultation.

He shook his head. 'You have nothing to thank me for, Genevra.' He lifted her hand and pressed it to his cheek, covering it there with his own. Pain flickered over his expression before determination banished it. 'I'll give you all the world can offer. You'll never want for anything again.'

She smiled, her eyes adoring him for his boundless generosity. 'I only want you, Christian.'

He drew in a sharp breath and slid her hand to his mouth, pressing fervent little kisses across her palm. Genevra's stomach contracted. She wanted him now, wanted to smother him with kisses and make him feel as precious to her as she was to him, wanted to hold him in her arms and love him with all that she was.

'Christian...'

It was a husky plea which he instantly answered, rising to his feet, holding her chair, taking her arm, linking her to him with a caring possessiveness that warmed her very soul.

The urgency of her desire melted into a wonderful sense of well-being. There was no need for haste. Christian would never leave her. From now on, he would always be at her side. She hugged closer to him as they walked up to their room, revelling in the security of their togetherness.

Christian either sensed her change of mood or felt the same need to savour this moment of total commitment to each other. He kissed her with a tenderness that twisted her heart, and Genevra knew that tonight there would be no rush to passion. Tonight they would know each other in every possible way.

'I love you,' she whispered, and kissed him with a soft reverence that expressed her total awareness of the man he was.

Their undressing was slow and deliberate, a conscious revelation of their bodies to each other. They touched, kissed, caressed, savouring every sensual nuance of being together. Only when their control moved from exquisite pleasure to painful need did they surrender to the ultimate mating of their bodies; melting into each other, fusing into one entity, exulting in the union that was so uniquely theirs.

Not the slightest shadow of doubt clouded Genevra's happiness as she lay in Christian's arms, his body curved around hers like a cradle of warm security. This love was real. Christian would never desert her or betray her as Luke had done. No amount of money in the whole world could buy him away from her. He would always be hers.

## CHAPTER TEN

THE next morning, Genevra felt she had been reborn to a new life. A little smile of irony curved her mouth as she noticed Christian's passport on the bedside table, lying next to his wallet and key-case. An American passport. If only she had looked for it a fortnight ago... but it didn't matter now. Better that she hadn't, or she might not have learned to love Christian as she did.

He was still shaving. More out of idle curiosity than a need for information, Genevra picked up the passport and opened it. The photograph was a grim-looking one, and she wrinkled her nose at it. Christian was much more handsome when he smiled. Place of birth—Rochester.

'Where's Rochester?' she asked as he emerged from the bathroom.

'On the U.S. side of Lake Ontario.'

'Is it nice?'

He shrugged. 'Haven't been there since I was a little kid. And talking about kids...' His face lit up with a grin of pure pleasure. '...I'm looking forward to telling ours the good news.'

Genevra laughed from sheer happiness. 'I know Johnny will be ecstatic. What about Felicity?'

'She'll think all her Christmases have come at once.'

And, indeed, when they returned to St Ives later that morning and broke the news to the children, both Johnny and Felicity could hardly contain their excitement. Apparently they had talked the matter over between themselves, both envying each other's parent and secretly wanting to belong to the one family. Auntie May, of course, clucked over all of them like a smug mother hen, saying again and again that she had known everything would work out right.

Christian took them all to lunch at Tregenna Castle. The children were too excited to have an afternoon nap, and they played around the grounds while the adults relaxed in deck-chairs on the front lawn. Eventually they all strolled down to the waterfront to have fish and chips for tea, and Felicity insisted that she stay overnight again with Johnny. Christian and Genevra tucked both their children into bed and gave them goodnight kisses, much to their wriggling delight.

'Will it always be like this now, Daddy?' Felicity asked hopefully, her eyes shining at Genevra with shyly possessive love.

'Always, sweetheart,' Christian promised her.

'I've wished and wished for a mummy,' she whispered to Genevra.

'And I've wished for a daughter, just like you,' Genevra whispered back, and Felicity breathed a sigh of huge contentment as she snuggled into her pillow.

A question about Christian's ex-wife flitted across Genevra's mind, but Johnny's more boisterous goodnight distracted her from it. The rest of the evening was spent with Auntie May, discussing plans for the future.

Christian was all for getting married as soon as possible, even though it would take some time to settle up Genevra's business. They talked about where they might live, without coming to any definite conclusion. Christian had leased a house in Eaton Square in London, and they would take up residence there initially.

Auntie May retired early, tactfully leaving the two lovers alone, but Christian didn't stay long. They were both tired, and Genevra insisted she had to work in the morning. She was yawning as she climbed the attic stairs to her bedroom, yet once she was between the sheets her mind was still too full of the day's events for sleep to come easily.

When she heard the soft, whimpering noises, Genevra did not at first connect them to a child, but as they began to be punctuated with sobs she suddenly realised they were coming from Johnny's bedroom. In an instant she was out of bed and flying across the landing. She found Felicity crouched into a huddle, her little body shaking with sobs.

Alarmed by the inexplicable distress, Genevra scooped her up in her arms and cradled her like a baby, making soft, soothing sounds as she carried her out of Johnny's room and into her own.

'G'evra...'

'Yes, darling. Were you having a bad dream?' Genevra asked, climbing into bed and cuddling her close for comfort.

'G'evra, I don't want you to die and go to heaven,' the little girl pleaded brokenly.

'I'm not going to die, Felicity,' Genevra assured her, wondering what fear had conjured up such a thought.

'But mummies want to have babies and...' she sucked in a long, quivering breath '...you'll die. And I want to keep you.'

'That won't happen, Felicity, I promise you.'

But not even the promise consoled the child. She looked up at Genevra, her huge eyes brimming with tears. 'My mummy had to die to get me born.'

Somehow, Genevra managed to swallow the shock of that bald statement, and spoke as calmly as she could. 'Who told you that, Felicity?'

'Daddy.' Another deep breath and the whole story came pouring out in jerky little bursts. 'He said Mummy wasn't strong enough to have a baby, but she wanted me so much that she had me anyway. He said I was more important than anything else to Mummy, and that's why she called me Felicity. 'Cause that means happiness. And I gave Mummy a lot of happiness when I was born. But I want a Mummy who's here, G'evra, not in heaven.'

The tearful plea was so heart-wrenching that Genevra felt tears prick her own eyes, but she firmly blinked them away and set about explaining that not all mothers died when they had babies, citing herself and Johnny as an obvious example. However, it took a lot of talking to banish Felicity's fear and, even when the little girl finally fell into a contented sleep, Genevra kept her in her own bed for extra reassurance.

She herself lay awake for a long time, pondering Christian's first marriage. She wondered what had been wrong with Felicity's mother. The child had been too distressed for Genevra to ask, but it was a tantalising question in Genevra's mind. Few women died from childbirth these days, and even fewer women knowingly put their lives at risk to have a child.

More important than anything else, Felicity had said. More important than her husband and the love they had supposedly shared? Genevra knew which choice she would have made. She would have lived for Christian and remained childless.

The choice Felicity's mother had made, and her subsequent death, would almost certainly have left deep emotional scars on Christian. Little wonder that he had never wanted to talk about his marriage. And Genevra recalled his concern over her getting pregnant that first night at the Manoir...perhaps he harboured the same irrational fear as his daughter, and wouldn't want to have any more children. That was something they hadn't discussed, and Genevra decided it needed talking about. But not in front of Felicity. It would have to wait until tomorrow night.

The next morning, Genevra started taking an inventory of the shop contents. She wondered if she should have a closing-down sale, or if a buyer would want to take over the stock with the business. Since she didn't know the legalities of selling leases, she telephoned Matthew Hastings for his advice.

'Matthew, Christian and I are going to get married,' she announced, imagining his delighted smile.

'Splendid! I am very happy for you, Genevra. Any chance of my meeting the chap?'

'Of course. I'd like you take the place of my father at the wedding,' she said impulsively.

She heard him clear his throat, and knew he was deeply touched by the request. 'I'd be honoured,' he said with deep sincerity.

Genevra felt an extra glow of happiness. Matthew had always been like a father to her. 'I'll let you know the date as soon as we've fixed it. Meanwhile...'

She explained what she needed to know about the bookshop, and Matthew outlined the various options open to her. When they had covered everything to their satisfaction, Genevra started to thank him, but Matthew interrupted her.

'Genevra...' He hesitated a moment, and there was a faint note of disquiet in his tone as he continued. 'That information you wanted on Anna Christie came in this morning. It's...umm...rather curious.'

'Oh?' Genevra prompted.

'Anna Christie was the maiden name of Luke Stanford's mother. The trust wasn't actually set up by her at all. She died twenty-four years ago. The Canadian solicitor received his instructions from an Australian solicitor, and those documents were signed by Luke Stanford himself.'

'But why?' It all seemed so convoluted; Genevra was at a loss to understand Luke's motives.

'Well, he obviously used his mother's name to keep himself distanced from you, but it appears that he wasn't quite the rotter I thought him. Even if it was only a feeling of guilt that prompted him into it, he went to a great deal of trouble to see that you would never be in any financial want. Of course, he could afford it easily enough, but it was decent of him. Most people wouldn't have bothered.'

Blood money, Genevra thought with angry bitterness. Luke had sold her out for millions and set up a trust fund of fifty thousand pounds to appease his conscience. She was glad now that she had used so little of it on herself. She didn't want anything from Luke Stanford.

But Johnny had a right to that money. As Luke's son, he had every right to it, and she would see that every penny of it was kept for him from now on.

'Genevra? You're not worrying about this, are you?' Matthew asked anxiously.

'No. I was just thinking that it really is Johnny's inheritance. I always had a funny feeling that it was, somehow. Thanks for finding out for me, Matthew.'

'Since Luke Stanford never knew of his son's existence, I could argue that point with you, Genevra,' he said drily. 'However, he certainly owes Johnny something, and if you're happier to accept it on that basis...'

'I'd hand it over to the Red Cross rather than touch another penny of it myself,' she declared decisively. 'If you don't mind, Matthew, just keep reinvesting the interest for Johnny.'

'Well, I'm glad that's settled,' he said with satisfaction. 'And you'll let me know about the wedding...'

Genevra was only too happy to switch her mind back on to Christian. She did not want to think of Luke Stanford ever again. All her memories of him had been completely soured. The deception he had played on her was unforgivable, and she was doubly grateful that Christian had proved so worthy of her trust.

She did not get the chance to talk with him alone until after the children had been put to bed that night. He suggested a stroll around the harbour in the lingering twilight, and Genevra eagerly agreed. She needed to know what his attitude was towards having a family. As it turned out, no sooner had she broached the subject than he set her mind at rest.

'We'll have as many children as you want, Genevra,' he said, without even a glimmer of reserve.

'It won't worry you?' she queried.

'Of course not. Why should it?'

She hesitated, reluctant to remind him of his first wife, yet feeling she should mention what Felicity had told her. However, as she related the previous night's incident with his daughter, Christian's sudden tension was disquieting, and not until she had finished speaking did that tension ease.

'I'll talk to her. I didn't realise...' He stopped, his face taking on a look of grim determination.

'That's in the past, Genevra. I won't have anything marring our future. I'll make Felicity understand.'

'Christian, do be careful,' Genevra warned, troubled by his rather extreme attitude. 'It's only natural that Felicity is affected by what happened to her mother.'

'We all were,' he muttered darkly, then in an abrupt change of mood he smiled at her. 'Don't worry about it, Genevra. She'll get over it fast enough. All Felicity needs, and all *I* need, is to be with you. You're a miracle for both of us.'

She relaxed and laughed. 'I think you're the miracle-worker. Do you realise we've only known each other for about three weeks?'

He shook his head. 'We knew each other in another life. We just re-met, that's all.'

Her eyes danced teasingly at him. 'Do you really believe that?'

'Yes,' he replied gravely, then smiled. 'My heart knew you instantly.'

'That's a lovely thing to say,' she sighed, and snuggled her head on to his shoulder as they walked along the harbour wall.

'There's someone I want you to meet, Genevra,' Christian said, throwing her a slightly anxious glance. 'I hope you'll like him.'

'If you do, then I'm sure I shall,' she assured him with happy confidence.

'It's Felicity's grandfather. My . . . father-in-law.'

Genevra frowned over the relationship. 'Will he want to meet me, Christian?'

'Very much so. Jack knows all about you, Genevra. I should explain that he and I are very close. As I told you, my own parents are dead. And Jack's alone now too, except for me and Felicity. He took care of her when...when I couldn't. Given me every possible support over the last three years.'

Christian stopped walking and turned to her, his expression pleading for her understanding. 'He's been like a father to me, Genevra.'

Like Matthew to me, she thought, and smiled. 'I'm glad he stood by you, Christian, and I'll be very happy to meet him.'

His answering smile was full of relief. 'He could come down from London tomorrow. Would dinner tomorrow night be all right?'

'Fine!' she agreed. 'And there's someone I want you to meet, too...' And she told him about Matthew, and how kind he had been to her over the years.

Genevra had no ill-feeling of premonition over the forthcoming meeting with Christian's father-in-law. Quite clearly, he was anxious not to lose access to his granddaughter, and she could well understand that. If the man held no prejudice against her taking his dead daughter's place, then Genevra would accept him unconditionally, too.

Nevertheless, as she rode up to the Castle with Christian the next evening, she did feel slightly nervous, and hoped she would make a good impression on him. And she was aware that Christian also was a little apprehensive that the meeting should go off well. His hand was squeezing hers tightly as they entered the drawing-room where his father-in-law was waiting for them.

A big man instantly rose to his feet from an arm-chair near the window. He was well over six feet, broad-shouldered and barrel-chested. His hair was starkly white, above a face that was darkly tanned and weathered with lines that suggested many sorrows in his life. His smile was slightly wistful as his gaze travelled quickly over Genevra, but the brown eyes gave her an unreserved welcome.

'Genevra, this is my father-in-law...Jack Preston.'

Preston! Jack...John Preston? For a moment, Genevra's mind reeled. Common sense instantly argued there were probably thousands of Prestons in the world. She forced her hand out to take the one offered to her. 'How do you do, Mr Preston,' she said a little too stiffly, still rocked by the coincidence.

Her hand was engulfed warmly by his. 'Let's make that Jack. I'm delighted to meet you, Genevra, and even more delighted to have this opportunity to wish you every happiness for the future.'

It was a generous speech, but Genevra barely registered a word of it. He had spoken with an Australian accent. Not American...Australian! An Australian John Preston whose daughter had died three years ago!

All Genevra's bright, shining dreams of everlasting love splintered into the most devastating nightmare as the implications pounded her brain. In sheer, piercing horror she screamed, and the scream echoed into a moan of the most terrible anguish.

## CHAPTER ELEVEN

BOTH men stared at Genevra in blank shock, but she didn't care. She didn't care if the whole hotel staff came running to check on what was happening. She wouldn't have cared if there'd been a hundred people in the room starting up in alarm at the way she had screamed.

She snatched her hand out of Jack Preston's warm clasp and hugged it under her arm, out of reach. She was alone. Alone in a far more desperate way than she had ever been before. And these men had done it to her with their deceit and treachery.

'Genevra...' The man who had called himself Christian Nemo reached out to her. 'What's wrong?'

She recoiled from his touch. 'How could you?' she whimpered, lost for a moment in the pain he had given her. 'You should have told me! You should have...'

Then a bitter rage billowed over the pain, feeding off the cruel deception he had played on her. She was sure now, but she would put the matter beyond all doubt. She wheeled on Jack Preston, her eyes blazing with contempt as she flew into venomous attack. 'Tell me your daughter's name, Mr Preston.'

He frowned and shot a worried look at his son-in-law.

'Tell me, Mr Preston...' Genevra's voice sharpened with cutting savagery. 'Was it Victoria?'

'Genevra!' Christian's voice...Luke's voice... pleading for forbearance, but she ruthlessly shut him out as he had done to her four years ago.

'Answer me!' she commanded. 'It was Victoria, wasn't it?'

The old man's face sagged with pain. 'Yes, that's so, my dear. But we always called her Vickie.'

'Genevra...' A hand clutched her arm. 'Please, you must listen to me...'

She swung on the man to whom she had so foolishly given her love, and beat his arm away from her. She felt no love for him now. 'Lies...all lies!' she panted, shaken by a fury so deep that all she wanted was to wound as she had been wounded. 'They said you were dead! Killed in a plane crash! But it's all been one huge deception, hasn't it...' Her mouth twisted with vicious mockery as she hurled his real name at him. '...Luke Stanford!'

She could say it now without the slightest shadow of doubt. Luke Stanford...the man she had loved and lost, the man who had betrayed and deceived her and put her through a hell of uncertainty.

Matthew had been right about the name, Nemo. It did mean no one. Christian Nemo did not exist. He was Luke Stanford!

The face that had fooled her into believing him contorted with agonised denial. 'I'm not that man any more, Genevra. Isn't that plain enough? I did what was necessary, only what was necessary to free you from any tie you might feel to the past. How could I come to you after what happened?'

Genevra's rage weakened for a moment, allowing that he had suffered during their separation, but then she remembered her own suffering, which had all been so unnecessary if he had ever really thought of her instead of himself.

Her teeth gnashed as she scorned his explanation. 'How you belittle me! And the love I once bore you! Did you even stop to think what I felt when you denied who you were at the Dorchester Hotel?'

'I wanted your love. Not your pity. Do you think it was easy for me to hold back after all these years of craving for you?' He stepped forwards, grasping her roughly by the shoulders. 'Genevra, I love you. I...'

'No!' she screamed at him, twisting out of his hold and sweeping out an arm that vehemently dismissed his claim. 'You never loved me! You never did...' her shrill voice choked into an anguished sob '...or you wouldn't have left me and married

Vickie. You wouldn't have done all the things you
did...'

'Genevra, I couldn't have lived with myself if I
hadn't tried to give Vickie the love she wanted. We'd
lived together for so many years...'

'Then how could you promise me what you did?
How could you lead me on, make love to me...'

'Because I loved you,' came the fierce answer,
and he cupped her face to forcibly hold her attention. 'And Vickie left me no other choice. I had
to do my best to make her happy...'

'Make *her* happy!' Genevra repeated bitterly, and
the rage consumed her again. She threw her head
back in proud disdain and stepped away from him,
her eyes accusing him of base betrayal. 'I know
better than that, Luke! You did it for the money.
All the millions that her father offered you...'

'That's not true!' Jack Preston shouldered his
way vehemently into the argument, clutching her
arm to press his defence. 'Luke was always...'

'Get your hand off me!' Genevra seethed at him.
'You got your daughter what she wanted, and you
didn't care what it cost. Johnny and I were
expendable.'

He shook his head in pained protest. 'No, it
wasn't that way!'

'Oh, yes it was!' She backed away from him so
that both men were in her sights, and she attacked
with all the concentrated power of the pain they

had dealt her over the years, her voice lashing out at them like a scourging whip.

'The truth is that I was discarded to bear my child alone, while Luke was bedding his new wife and getting her pregnant. The truth is that she had all the security of marriage and wealth, all the care and attention, all the love...' She choked as tears of desolation brimmed her eyes.

'Genevra...please, please listen to me.'

She turned tortured eyes to the man she could never trust again. 'I waited for you, Luke. Waited to hear from you every day of four long, lonely years. I believed in our love. I made excuses for the silence. I wove fantasies to explain why you didn't come back to me.'

'I couldn't! Not until now,' he pleaded. 'I came as soon as I could offer you a reasonable kind of life.'

Her voice broke with anguish. 'You could have called me three years ago, Luke. I would have come. I would have accepted anything, forgiven you anything, just to be reunited with you. But my love wasn't enough for you. It came last on your list of priorities.'

'You were better off anywhere than with me!' he cried in violent denial.

'Yes. Better off without you,' Genevra agreed, a deathly numbness spreading through her. She looked at him with bleak, wintry eyes. 'That's what

Matthew told me when the report from the inquiry agent came back. You see, Luke, the waiting and the silence from you had gone on too long. I couldn't bear not knowing what had happened to you, so I asked my solicitor to find out. And then I knew... I knew how deeply you had betrayed me.'

His hands reached out to her in despairing appeal. 'Genevra, I didn't know about Johnny. I didn't want to make the choice I did...'

'You didn't think of me, Luke. You *never* thought of me!'

'It was only the thought of you that kept me alive. I swear to you...'

She flapped her hands in despairing rejection as he started towards her. 'No more lies, Luke. No more deception. I don't know how you did it—the colour of your eyes, the American passport, and all the other things. I don't even know *why* you did it. And I don't care any more. I never want to see you again.'

'You don't mean that, Genevra,' he begged in a hoarse, driven voice.

'Yes, I do. I can't take any more. And I'm not going to. You cheated me. And you cheated Johnny.'

She closed her eyes to the haunted look on his face and turned her back on him, moving her trembling legs towards the doorway.

'No!' Rough hands caught her and spun her around. His arms imprisoned her in a vicelike embrace, as his face worked to bring turbulent emotion under control. 'I won't let you do this. I love you, Genevra. And you love me. We've got to talk this out and put it behind us. You can't walk away from me now.'

'You did, Luke,' she reminded him, too soul-sickened to answer any of his needs or desires. 'You walked away from me four years ago. And you never came back. Did you know what Nemo means, Luke? It means no one.'

'Stop it, Genevra!' He shook her in sheer desperation. 'We've got the rest of our lives together. You know you want that as much as I do.'

'Not any more. Let me go, Luke.'

He stared down at her, fighting the finality stamped on her cold, closed face. And slowly the fight drained out of him and his arms dropped away from her. 'I love you,' he said defeatedly. 'I tried...' He turned away from her, his shoulders slumped, his head turning helplessly from side to side. 'There just wasn't... a right choice.'

'Well, you certainly didn't make any of the right choices where I was concerned,' she said flatly, and on that note of fatal judgement she forced herself to walk away—out of his life, out of Tregenna Castle, along the hotel driveway to the path which led down to the village where she had lived all her life...before Luke, and after Luke.

At least that was constant.

The numbness wore off as she walked. Misery welled out of her soul, giving birth to inconsolable despair. How could she love a man who had practised so much deceit on her? And yet she knew that there would never be anyone else for her. Twice he had come into her life and stolen her heart. Just like a thief, uncaring of what damage he did, as long as he got what he wanted. A thief in disguise.

Tears blinded her, and when her foot caught a mossy patch on the path she almost slipped over. Shaken, and too upset to keep going, Genevra took temporary refuge on the slatted bench-seat that marked a resting-point for the steep pathway. Situated as it was under the trees, and surrounded by hydrangea bushes and other shrubs, it provided her with sorely needed privacy. It was too early to go home. She couldn't bear to face Auntie May tonight. Tomorrow would be soon enough to tell her the truth.

And what *was* the truth? Genevra wasn't sure of anything any more. The lies Luke had told her, the lies he had lived since he came back...nothing that he had said or done could be trusted. How could a happy, secure future be built on such a rotten foundation? How long had he meant to keep up the deception? If she hadn't known about John Preston, if she had married him . . .

A fresh gush of tears flowed down her cheeks, and she doubled over in anguished shame as she remembered all the times they had made love. Only it wasn't love. He didn't love her. She had given herself to a man who had never appreciated what she had given. He had put it aside until he felt a need for it. He had never cared about her needs.

The soft crunch of approaching footsteps drove her into a huddle at the furthest end of the bench-seat away from the path. Her heart beat a sickening protest as the person paused. She mentally begged whoever it was to go on, to leave her alone with her misery. The continuing silence was an added torture to her jagged nerves.

'Genevra, I have to speak to you.'

The Australian voice of Jack Preston was soft, but it fired a bitter turmoil of resentment through Genevra's aching heart. She turned a tear-streaked face to him. 'Go away. Just go away,' she sobbed, hating him for seeing her distress.

'I'm sorry, but I can't do that.' He slowly lowered himself on to the other end of the seat, his face set in grave lines of determination.

It was abundantly clear that he didn't intend to let her escape him. There was a formidable strength in his bearing that stifled any further protest from Genevra. She bit her lips and turned her head away, pointedly ignoring his presence, although it oppressed her further.

'Why can't you leave me alone? Haven't you done enough?' she demanded wearily.

His sigh was heavy. 'Luke is like a son to me, Genevra.'

'And I am nothing,' she said in painful derision.

'You're the key to the life I want him to have.'

'The key's been too abused for it to work any more, Mr Preston.'

'You've been badly hurt, Genevra, but believe me, Luke has walked a harder road than you to reach this point.'

She looked at him in scathing disbelief, but his gaze held hers steadily and with steely purpose. 'I've watched the woman I loved die. I've watched the daughter I loved die. I've watched Luke go through agonies that I wouldn't wish on my worst enemy. And I will not stand by now and let his one chance at happiness be destroyed by misunderstandings and misconceptions.'

He shook his head, as if burdened too heavily with what had to be revealed. 'I'll tell you the truth, Genevra, and when you've listened to all I have to say, then you can judge the man you've just rejected. I won't stop you if you still want to walk away. You have the right to decide your own destiny. But Luke deserves a fair hearing, and since you won't give it to him, I'm prepared to force it down your throat. If I have to.'

'And how will I know if it's the truth?' Genevra shot at him, although he had stirred a treacherous fever of curiosity with his claims.

He gave her a grim smile. 'Because nothing else will serve now.'

## CHAPTER TWELVE

GENEVRA slumped back in the seat and stared unseeingly at the greenery that enclosed herself and Jack Preston in a private little world. The trees formed a canopy above them. The shrubbery was so thick that one couldn't see the adjoining golf course, nor the village below. The sounds of civilisation were shut out, and an almost unnatural hush seemed to hang around them.

The tension slowly drained out of Genevra. She felt like a limp sponge waiting for the words that might or might not inject new life into her. She did not even feel hostile towards Jack Preston any more. He was simply there, an unknown entity that didn't really impinge on her life. Only his words could do that.

'Go ahead,' she invited listlessly. 'Talk all you want. I'm not going anywhere.'

'I hope you don't choose to live your life as I've had to live mine,' he said with a wealth of sadness. 'I'm considered a great success. Looked up to. Envied. But none of it—the success, the wealth or the power—nothing can compensate for the loss of the woman I loved.'

'Your wife?' Genevra asked, a little impatient with his philosophising. What possible bearing could his love-life have on her relationship with Luke Stanford?

'No. Anna Christie . . . Anna Christie Stanford,' he replied, his eyes suddenly swimming with tears.

Genevra quickly turned her head away, discomfited by the naked emotion.

'When I met Anna, she had already been married to Luke's father for ten years. My own marriage was over in any real sense. Only a few months after Vickie was born, my wife took a fall from her horse while show-jumping, and suffered such extensive brain damage that . . .' The clearing of his throat was harsh before he dragged out the brutal reality. 'She was in an eternal coma. They kept her alive on machines, but there was no hope of her ever recovering.'

'How terrible for you!' Genevra whispered sympathetically.

'You could not imagine . . . but at least I had Vickie to love. And then I met Anna.'

He paused, and Genevra sensed he could remember that moment as vividly as if it was happening now. There was a softness, a wonder, even awe in those last few words. He recollected himself and spoke on.

'I'd gone to the United States on business. Anna worked for a secretarial service. The moment I saw her... it was like instant recognition. A soul-mate. I cannot explain to you the power, the magic of meeting her eyes and...' His breath hissed out in a whisper of longing. 'But perhaps you do know how it feels... when it happens. I would have done anything for that woman. But she would not have me.'

His hands clenched, even now wanting to fight that decision. 'She loved me, I know she did. Although she would never admit it. She had said she could never leave her husband and son. I promised her I'd accept her son as my own, but there was a deep fear in her that she wouldn't explain... until it was too late.

'Vickie contracted scarlet fever and I had to fly home. Anna wrote and begged me not to come back. She said I would only cause her pain if I did.' He slumped forwards, propping his head in his hands. His voice came brokenly, half-muffled. 'I should have gone. Should have taken her and Luke way out of reach of the maniac she had married. Three months later, she wrote another letter, begging me to come.'

His shoulders hunched over further and Genevra sensed that he was weeping behind his covering hands. She sat there in helpless silence, knowing she could do nothing to appease his grief.

'She was in hospital with broken ribs, a punctured lung, and other internal injuries. He'd beaten her up. And her son, who had tried to protect her. I took the first flight that was possible, but by the time I got there Anna was barely hanging on to life. She asked me if I'd take Luke, bring him up as my boy. I promised I would. I had only a few hours with her and she just...just slipped away from me.'

He groped in a pocket for a handkerchief, and took his time blowing his nose. Genevra managed to stem her own tears by blinking hard. She felt so sorry for him...first his wife and then Anna. He expelled a shuddering breath and sagged back on to the bench-seat.

'Anna's husband couldn't be found. I took Luke home with me. He was nine years old, and very much his mother's son. Vickie was only two then, and in very delicate health. She was one of the unlucky ones. The scarlet fever had left her with complications, in this instance, acute nephritis, a kidney disease that circumscribed her life, making it impossible for her to lead a normal existence. I suppose both Luke and I always indulged her in our different ways.

'Luke was very protective of her, right from the beginning, and Vickie adored him. He looked after her, did all he could to keep her happy. We both did. Her life expectancy was not good. There were always health problems. I don't know when the love for her big brother changed to a womanly love.'

He rubbed his eyelids in a gesture of intense despair. Genevra said nothing, caught up in the story he was unfolding for her. She had seen how Luke was with Felicity and Johnny, and could well imagine how caring he would be to a frail little sister.

Jack Preston heaved a tired sigh and continued, 'Sometimes she showed a jealous possessiveness when Luke had casual attachments to other women, but he always laughed it off, saying she was the only important woman in his life. Apparently, Vickie was satisfied with that. Certainly, there were no serious love affairs to make her feel that her own secret desires were threatened. Until he came to England and met you, Genevra. It was obvious from his phone calls and letters that he was very serious about you.

'Vickie went into a depression that I couldn't shake her out of. She didn't take care of herself. She became so ill that she had to be rushed to hospital, and the doctors said she was refusing to cooperate with their treatment.

'I called Luke home. He was on his way when Vickie told me that she had nothing to live for any more. And she told me why.'

His hand lifted in a helpless little gesture. 'Luke was lost to her and she wanted to die. By that time, she'd done so much irreversible damage to herself that even with the greatest possible care, she would only live a few more years.'

His eyes sought Genevra's, pleading for her understanding. 'You spoke truly a little while ago when you said you were nothing to me. You were only a name, and I didn't care about you. Vickie had such little time left. I wanted her to have her heart's desire before she died. I begged Luke to give himself to her for that time, to give her the fulfilment of her dreams. He could go back to you afterwards.'

His mouth turned down in a grimace of self-abasement. 'I demanded things of him that should not be demanded of anyone. I used every piece of emotional blackmail I could think of to force his hand. But in the end, it was his own love for Vickie that forced the choice. He didn't love her as he loved you, Genevra, but he made Vickie believe he did for the fifteen months that she lived.'

Tears filled Genevra's eyes as she remembered the words Luke had written to her so long ago. 'I cannot turn my back on the love and obligations I owe my family. I could not be happy within myself, nor could I make you happy, knowing I had refused to answer their needs when they have given me so much.'

She wished he had written the whole truth, but she understood it now. She even understood why he had felt he didn't have the right to ask her to wait for him while he spent the intervening period making another woman feel loved.

'Money never entered into it, Genevra. The partnership papers had been drawn up while Luke was in England. It had always been planned that he would eventually take over the business from me. He is my son in everything but name. It was pure coincidence that the legalities were finalised at the time of his marriage to Vickie. Money would never have persuaded Luke, anyway. He's not the kind of person that can be bought.'

Genevra believed him, but it was a blessed relief to have it spelled out so convincingly. Her instincts had told her Matthew was wrong. She should have been guided by them, instead of accepting Matthew's pragmatic interpretation of the facts.

'I think you know that Vickie died in giving birth to Felicity?'

'Yes,' Genevra whispered, too choked up to answer more firmly.

'She was determined to have a baby. It was a nine-month suicide. She refused to have an abortion to prolong her life. She lived just long enough to hold Felicity in her arms. She died happy, as if there could be no greater fulfilment for having lived.'

He paused and took a deep breath. 'I was shocked when Luke told me he'd booked a flight to England a few weeks later. It was so soon after...but one look in his eyes and I knew there was no stopping him. I hadn't realised until then what you meant to him. He was desperate for you, Genevra.'

'The plane he boarded was to take him from Muswellbrook, where we had a power station under construction, to Mascot Airport in time to link with his international flight to London. I saw Luke on to the plane and watched it take off. It suddenly faltered in the air. Flames burst out of one engine. The plane nosedived to the ground and exploded.'

He shook his head, his face etched in appalled memory of the scene. 'I don't know how Luke survived the crash. No one else did.'

'The newspaper report sent by my inquiry agent stated that no one survived,' Genevra told him, half asking for an explanation of the inaccuracy.

His mouth made an ironic grimace. 'Luke was pronounced dead on arrival at the hospital. If a reporter had a deadline to meet, he wouldn't have bothered rechecking later. And it was a small plane crash. Yesterday's news. I didn't even look at newspapers while Luke was in such a critical state, so I didn't see the report. Even if I had, I doubt I would have asked for a correction. At the time, Luke could have taken his last breath at any minute. I'm sorry, Genevra.'

'It's not your fault,' she sighed, thinking that the inquiry agent could have done a bit more checking. 'But I don't understand how Luke could be pronounced dead if he wasn't.'

'He had terrible injuries. He looked...
unrecoverable. I rode with him in the ambulance
to the hospital. The paramedics kept working on
him all the way. His heart stopped as they wheeled
him into the casualty ward, but I wouldn't let the
doctors give up on him, despite what they told me.
Despite what I could see for myself. I needed Luke
to live.

'They hammered his chest and got his pulse
working again. Then the rest had to be attended
to. His face was cut open and burnt. One eye completely gone, the other's sight affected by the fire.
His body was broken in so many places that he was
in hospital for months before he could even be
moved. They said he'd never walk again.'

'My God!' Genevra breathed, horrified by the
toll of injuries. 'If only he'd sent for me. I could
have...'

'No, Genevra! He was in enough trauma as it
was. Your presence would have been an additional
torment. He couldn't have borne it.'

'Why?' she cried in protest. 'At least I could have
given him emotional support.'

'Or emotional torture?' came the pointed reply.

Genevra frowned at him in non-comprehension.

'Luke was crippled,' came the harsh reminder.
'He couldn't make love to you. He was helpless,
disfigured, his life hopelessly changed from what
it had been when you fell in love with him. And

he had given up all claim to your love by marrying Vickie. How could he possibly ask you to come to him under those circumstances? Would you have asked it of him if the situation was reversed?'

Genevra paused to think through what she might have felt. Despair...utter despair. And no...she would never have called him, no matter how desperately she might have wanted to. Luke had not been selfish, after all. Had never been selfish in all the time she had known him. He had given everything in his love for her and for Vickie.

Genevra looked up at Jack Preston and shook her head. Understanding was slowly penetrating, and not for a moment did she doubt that he was telling her anything but the unvarnished truth. 'I would have done what Luke did. Fought it out alone.'

'As you did, my dear,' the old man said quietly. 'Don't think I don't appreciate what you've been through. When Anna chose to stay with her husband... I know the burning ache of loss all too well.'

The compassion in his eyes reached into Genevra, and in that instant they knew each other and a close bond of understanding was forged. 'How did Luke recover from his paralysis?' she asked softly.

'I took him to a neuro-surgery clinic in America. I couldn't even begin to enumerate the operations he suffered through so that he could walk again.

One leg ended up shorter than the other. So he followed through a hell of a program to stretch it back to size. There's still a weakness that forces him to use a walking-stick occasionally.'

'He hasn't used it at all since that afternoon at the Dorchester,' Genevra observed thoughtfully. 'Maybe his leg is stronger now.'

A musing little smile was thrown at her. 'The power of love.'

Genevra flushed and quickly redirected the conversation. 'How long did all the healing take?'

'Until very recently. You see, the cosmetic surgery to his face took years...taking bone from his hips...skin grafts...and the corneal graft on his eye...it seemed never-ending. He still has to wear a tinted lens to reduce glare.'

'Oh!' she breathed. 'So that's why...'

'His eye colour looks different? Yes. And, as for the American passport, Luke was born an American citizen and still is. He changed his name by deed-poll. All perfectly legal.' His mouth took on an ironic twist. 'I'm afraid I haven't got used to it yet. He's been Luke to me for far too long.'

'Why Christian?' Genevra asked.

'He's never said. I think perhaps it's a twist of his mother's name. Anna Christie—Christian. He loved her very much.'

She nodded, thinking of the Anna Christie Trust. Luke had done what he could to solve her financial difficulties over the bookshop and ensure that she would never be in any real want until he could come back to her. He had not really deserted her. Or deceived her. Except over his actual identity.

'Why did he come back as Christian Nemo, instead of as Luke?'

'He said he didn't want any emotional pressures hanging over from the past. And he's not the same man he was, Genevra. Too much has happened. And too much time had passed for him to be at all confident of your love. After all, he had broken his promises to you and married someone else. He felt he had no right to expect anything from you.'

He gave a dry little smile. 'If you want my opinion, he was afraid that you would reject him out of hand. As you did tonight. But if you fell in love with Christian Nemo...to have you, Genevra, he would have been Christian Nemo for the rest of his life.'

The smile drooped into a sad grimace. 'He told you the truth, you know. It was only the thought of you that kept him alive, that drove him to suffer through all he suffered so he could come back to you as a man who could give you the kind of life he wanted to give you. And that is love, Genevra. The deepest kind of love a man can feel. And give.'

She heaved a long sigh, expelling the last lingering doubt from her heart. 'I've been a terrible fool, haven't I?'

'No. I thought Luke was foolish to take the course he did. The truth is best. If Anna had told me the truth about her husband's violent nature...'

He sighed too, then reached over and took Genevra's hand, pressing it in a comforting way. 'You do love him, don't you?'

'Yes.'

'Then I think you should go back to him now, Genevra. He's been through too much. If you let him keep thinking he's lost you...'

Her heart leapt with fear. Christian—Luke—had said he would not want to live without her. 'I've got to run,' she gasped, jumping to her feet and pulling her hand free. 'Thank you...thank you for everything!' she called back as she flew up the path.

He answered something, but her heart was pounding too loudly for her to decipher the words, and she could not stop. She had to get to Luke as fast as her legs would carry her.

## CHAPTER THIRTEEN

GENEVRA'S mind whirled through the possibilities as she ran. Luke would not have stayed in the drawing-room where she had left him. Her gaze darted around the grounds, but there was no unaccompanied man in sight, and she was almost certain he would seek the privacy of his room. Or Felicity's.

A child was a reason for living. Johnny had been her only consolation throughout the four lonely years she had waited for Luke. Her son had given her life some meaning. Even though Felicity was down in the village with Johnny, Luke might have gone into her adjoining hotel room in an instinctive need to feel he had some purpose left to fulfil.

Genevra ran down the wide reception hallway, ignoring the startled exclamations of the staff on duty at the desk. She pounded up the stairs and virtually threw herself at the door to Luke's room, thumping it with both hands as she called his name in high-pitched agitation.

The door was not opened. There was no audible reply. Genevra propelled herself to the next door and banged on it with all her might, pleading with

Luke to let her in, but again there was no answer to her frantic attempts to reach him.

Genevra could not believe that Luke would completely ignore her. He wasn't here. She felt no sense of his presence behind these walls. She leaned against the door to Felicity's room, her forehead pressed to the panelling as she tried to think where else to look for him.

Her mind was too jammed with fear to come up with any answers. In a frantic need to do something, Genevra rushed back down to the reception desk. 'Have you seen Mr Nemo in the last hour or so?' she demanded sharply.

The two men raised their eyebrows at each other and shook their heads in unison. 'We only came on duty ten minutes ago, madame,' the older man replied. 'Would you like me to call his room?'

'No...no...' Genevra answered distractedly and turned away, feeling totally bereft.

Where? Where would he go? She was afraid to ask herself what he would do, but the question edged through the fear as she walked blindly out of the hotel. Reverse the position, she told herself... what would she do? And instantly the answer flashed into her mind. Felicity!

Of course, he would not leave his daughter in Genevra's home after that bitterly total condemnation of him and his kin. She had said she never wanted to see him again, and by association that meant Felicity, too. Guilt and shame wrung Genevra's heart as she thought of the little girl's bewilderment and distress at being abruptly removed from a home where she had finally felt emotionally secure. If it was not already too late, she had to stop Luke from doing it.

She hesitated a moment, undecided whether to take the pathway which was a quicker route to the village, or take the road in case Luke was already in a taxi on his way back to the hotel with Felicity. She did not want to miss him, yet she didn't want to waste any precious minutes, either. Genevra was still dithering when Jack Preston rounded the corner of the hotel, and the sight of him inspired a better idea.

'Mr Preston, did you drive a car to St Ives?' she asked, pouncing on him in anxious haste.

'Yes. It's parked around here.' He waved in the direction from whence he had just come.

'Please, will you drive me down to the village? I've got to get home as fast as I can. I suspect Luke's gone there to pick up Felicity.'

To Genevra's mind it was almost a certainty, not a suspicion. Her intuition had never played her false where Luke was concerned. Hadn't she known from his letter that he wanted her to wait for him? Hadn't she known Christian Nemo was Luke, despite all the evidence to the contrary? She could not be wrong about his intentions now! It was only the timing that could go wrong. She desperately hoped that she wouldn't be too late. Not now, when everything her life meant depended on it.

Jack Preston did not pause to question. He moved swiftly, leading her straight to a Daimler and settling them both into it with an economy of action for which Genevra was intensely grateful. 'You will have to direct me,' was all he said as he headed the car towards the exit from the hotel grounds.

They met no taxi on the way. Genevra anxiously scanned the footpaths and narrow lanes for a man with a little girl, but there was no such couple in sight. Jack Preston parked the Daimler just outside the bookshop. 'I'll wait for you,' he said.

'Luke has to be here!' Genevra said on a tight, frantic note, and dashed out of the car, the shop-key ready in her hand. Once inside the shop, with the door relocked behind her, Genevra paused to take a deep, steadying breath, and in that momentary silence she heard the thud of the upstairs door being firmly closed, then footsteps coming down the staircase to the shop. She froze, tension screaming along every nerve.

He walked slowly, heavily, his head bent broodingly over the sleeping child in his arms. It was not until he stepped on to the shop-floor that he glanced up and saw Genevra. His whole body stiffened to a halt, and the dark pain on his face wrung Genevra's heart.

'I was just...getting Felicity,' he said with a strained catch in his voice. 'I'll be going now,' he added in a bare whisper.

'I'm sorry,' Genevra rushed out. 'You mustn't go! What I said up there...'

He was shaking his head. 'I can see now what I did to you. I'm not going to hurt you any further, Genevra.'

His mouth twisted into a bleak grimace. 'There are some broken pieces of life that can never be put back together, no matter how desperate the need is. I should have left you alone. I'm sorry.'

'No! I wanted you to come back, Luke. I never wanted anything so desperately. I've never loved any other man. I never will,' Genevra pleaded, frightened by his retreat from her.

He winced, as though her claim turned a knife in an agonising wound. 'Genevra, I can't take back what's been done, and if I had the choice again, I couldn't do any differently. Vickie...'

His gaze fell to the small bundle of humanity he held in his arms. 'She was even younger than Felicity when Jack took me into his home. She was...very dear to me. I couldn't let her down...not when she was going to die...not when she needed me so badly.' His arms tightened convulsively around the child, and he lifted a face which was engraved with years of agony. 'I did what I had to.'

'I know,' she said softly. 'It was the right choice, Luke. The only choice.'

'Genevra...' Need and despair roughened his voice. 'I wish...I wish we hadn't met until now.'

'Then we wouldn't have Johnny, would we? Or Felicity,' she reminded him, walking down the shop to where he stood, then lovingly caressing the little girl's baby-soft cheek. 'Would you really wish that, Luke?'

He seemed stunned, unable to accept what her words and actions implied. Felicity stirred in his arms and opened her eyes.

'G'evra...' she murmured sleepily.

'Yes, darling?'

'Can I come into bed with you?'

Genevra smiled down at her. 'Not right now, Felicity. But your Daddy and I will tuck you into your bed and kiss you goodnight. And in the morning you can come into my bed. Will that do?'

'Mmm,' she sighed contentedly.

Genevra looked up at the man she loved, her eyes imploring his forgiveness for her hasty judgements. 'My need for you is as great as Vickie's ever was. You're not going to let me down now, are you, Luke?'

'You still...want me, Genevra?' he asked incredulously.

'Till the day I die, and beyond,' she answered with vehement conviction. 'I'm sorry for all the cruel things I said to you. I was terribly wrong about everything. Can you forgive me?'

'Forgive you?' he choked. 'It's I who should be asking...'

'No.' She placed a hushing finger to his lips. 'I'm glad you gave Vickie that time, Luke. We have so many years ahead of us, I'll never begrudge her that brief happiness, I promise you. As for the rest, I'm just thankful that you did come back to me, under any name.'

'You really mean this, Genevra?' he breathed, hardly daring to believe her.

'With all my heart. I love you too much to ever let you go again,' she said simply.

Naked yearning throbbed from him as relief and desire furred his speech. 'I never stopped loving you...thinking of you...wanting you with me...'

She touched the child he was still clutching tightly. 'Let's put Felicity to bed. Then we can discuss...whatever is necessary,' she said, but her eyes promised a far more expressive way of communicating their need for each other.

Genevra led the way upstairs. She surprised Auntie May, pacing the living-room floor and wearing a harried expression. 'Genevra!' she cried. 'Christian came and...' Her gaze lifted to the man who had followed her niece. 'Oh! You've come back!'

Genevra gave her aunt a comforting hug. 'Not to worry. Nothing's wrong. We had a . . . a tiny misunderstanding, that's all,' she explained quickly.

'Oh!' Auntie May sagged with relief. 'I thought...well, never mind. Is there anything I can do for you?'

Genevra suddenly remembered Jack Preston, waiting outside in the Daimler.

She described him to Auntie May, and asked her to let him know that there were no more problems. Christian and Felicity were here.

Auntie May's normal air of good cheer returned as she said she'd be only too happy to have a little chat with Felicity's grandfather; and off she went, obviously pleased to have such a message to deliver.

Christian carried Felicity up the stairs to Johnny's attic bedroom, and Genevra tucked her into bed. As she bent to kiss the little girl goodnight, Felicity's arms reached out and curled possessively around her neck.

'Are you my mummy now, G'evra?'

The whispered plea held a plaintive need that tugged at Genevra's heart. She lifted Felicity up, hugging her with reassuring fervour. 'Yes, I am. And Johnny's your brother. And we're always going to be a family.' Her eyes met Luke's over Felicity's head. 'She needs so much love.'

'We both do,' he answered huskily.

'Let's take her into my bed for a while. We'll always have each other, Luke.'

'Yes.' He smiled, and the warm glow of that smile filled Genevra with the richest happiness of all.

'Mummy? Is Felicity sick?'

They turned quickly to Johnny who had hitched himself up in his bed.

'No. She just wanted a cuddle,' Luke told him and swung him out of bed, lifting him high in squealing delight before planting him on his broad shoulder.

They grinned at each other, father and son sharing an indulgent awareness of a girl's need for cuddles. 'Do you think you and I could fit into Mummy's bed, too?' Luke asked laughingly.

'Yes!' Johnny crowed.

So they all bundled into Genevra's bed, the children in the middle and their parents stretched out on either side of them. Luke told them stories and, underneath the pillows, his hand found Genevra's and gripped tight.

This is what life is all about, Genevra thought with blissful contentment: to be with the man she loved, sharing a happy time with their children, forging a bond that would never be shaken again. Her fingers squeezed his, and their eyes met without any of the doubt and pain that had shadowed the past. Their togetherness was complete and secure.

## CHAPTER FOURTEEN

EVERYTHING had worked out perfectly, Genevra thought with a happy glow of satisfaction. All she had to do was sign the contract Matthew had ready, and her last personal responsibility for her single life would be discharged. The bookshop and residence at St Ives would pass to the new owner.

She and Johnny and Auntie May had already moved to the house Luke had leased in Eaton Square. Of course, it was a big jump from their old life in the village, but there were no regrets.

Johnny was enchanted with London, and this morning Luke had taken him and Felicity for a Thames boat-ride to Greenwich to see the Cutty Sark, which Luke had informed them was one of the fastest sailing ships ever made.

And the most extraordinary thing of all—Auntie May and Jack Preston were obviously finding a new lease of life in each other's company. 'A fine gentleman,' Auntie May had pronounced the morning after she had met him. But now it was, 'That Jack Preston is a lovely man, Genevra. He needs someone to look after him.' And Jack was looking ten years younger with the 'looking after' Auntie May was giving him.

Genevra couldn't help grinning to herself as she mounted the stairs to Matthew's chambers, but there was one sobering thought at the back of her mind. She still had to tell Matthew about Christian Nemo's real identity.

After Genevra's business was settled, Luke was meeting them both for lunch at the Dorchester Hotel, and Genevra didn't want Matthew under any delusions about the man she loved.

She recalled Auntie May's initial confusion over the situation, but Auntie May had been so enamoured of Christian Nemo that, if he was Luke Stanford, they were both fine men and couldn't do any wrong. It had all been 'an unfortunate tragedy' and 'all's well that ends well'.

Genevra doubted that Matthew would take quite the same simplistic view as Auntie May, but he wouldn't be able to argue with the facts she gave him. And he had said he wanted her to be happy. If he could not see she was brimming over with happiness then he would have to be blind.

And Matthew was certainly not blind when his secretary ushered Genevra into his office. He rose instantly to greet her, his shrewd blue eyes twinkling with appreciation. 'I've never seen you look so lovely, Genevra! Positively blooming!' he said with a beaming smile.

Genevra laughed and gave him an affectionate kiss.

He took her hands, pressing them in delighted approval. 'I am very much looking forward to meeting this man who's put such a beautiful sparkle in your eyes.'

'Yes . . . well, I think *you'd* better sit down this time, Matthew, because I have something to tell you and I don't want you fainting on me,' Genevra said teasingly.

The eyebrows arched in a good-humoured, quizzical fashion. It was obvious from Genevra's mood and manner that any shock she might deliver could not be an unpleasant one. 'Just as well I asked Beverley to bring in a tea-tray,' he observed drily.

He saw Genevra settled in a comfortable chair before resuming his own, then gestured an invitation for her to enlighten him.

'You remember that day I asked you to find out about Luke Stanford?'

Matthew nodded.

'I went from here to the Dorchester to meet Christian. I saw a man walking down the Promenade Room, and from the back view I was certain he was Luke.'

'Good heavens!' Matthew exclaimed, his eyebrows lowering into a frown of sympathetic concern.

Genevra smiled. 'I raced after him, but when he turned around his face was different. It bore the scars of a terrible accident, and the nose and jawline were the wrong shape. He introduced himself as Christian Nemo, which completely rattled me.'

Her mouth curved in whimsical remembrance. 'But the touch of his hand, his voice, and his smile were so like Luke's that, by the time I left him that afternoon, I was certain that Christian Nemo was really Luke Stanford, and that he had stayed away from me all those years because something dreadful had happened to him.'

'Oh, my dear! No wonder you were shocked when I told you Luke Stanford was dead,' Matthew said in quick sympathy.

'Yes. But he wasn't dead, Matthew. Christian is Luke.'

His jaw dropped open and his secretary timed her entrance with the tea-tray to perfection. Genevra got up and served Matthew while he recovered himself. Then she told him all about Luke's marriage to Vickie and the plane crash which had delayed his return for so many years.

'Then it wasn't the money?' Matthew observed, shaking his head in bemusement over the whole affair.

Genevra grinned at him. 'The trouble with you, Matthew, is that you've seen too much greed, envy, hatred, and malice.'

He laughed. 'Well, I'm very happy they didn't apply in this case.'

Genevra's grin dropped into a grimace. 'Except for me. I almost messed everything up. When Christian introduced me to Jack Preston, I knew the inquiry agent had been wrong about Luke's death, and I turned on him, accusing him of the basest treachery. I was so jealous of Vickie and all that he'd given her while I...' She gave a wry shrug. 'You know what I mean.'

He nodded gravely. 'I'm sorry, Genevra. I certainly didn't do you a good turn in getting that information to you, or interpreting it as I did.'

'Yes, you did,' Genevra corrected him quickly. 'It forced the truth into the open. And Matthew...I really learnt something important. You're a much better and happier person if you think of others instead of yourself. Luke is such a wonderful human being. I'm so lucky to have him back.'

Matthew's mouth curved into a whimsical smile. 'I'm of the opinion that he's lucky to have you back, Genevra. If I were thirty years younger, I might have contested his claim on you.'

Genevra's eyes danced appreciation of the compliment. 'I'm afraid I would have disappointed you, Matthew. There's only ever been one man for me. Christian or Luke—the name didn't matter—I loved him from the very first meeting.'

And her love was such a live, vibrant thing that it held Matthew in awed silence for several moments. 'He is a very lucky man,' he finally sighed.

'You'll soon see what a wonderful person he is,' Genevra assured him. 'And you will be free for our wedding day next week?' she added anxiously.

'I've cleared the day of all appointments. Even ordered a new morning-coat.'

She happily related all the wedding and honeymoon plans. Matthew kept nodding benevolently, finding enormous pleasure in the play of joyful anticipation on Genevra's face. He eventually drew her attention to the documents which needed her signature. She didn't bother reading them, and for once he did not insist. After all, he had prepared them himself and, as always, had been meticulous in looking after Genevra's interests.

And it did his heart good to see her with the man she loved when they lunched together at the Dorchester. By the time he left them, he no longer harboured any reservations about her husband-to-be. Genevra would be safe with him. 'To love and to cherish...' the words from the marriage service ran through his mind and he smiled to himself.

A week later, he listened to Luke Stanford repeating them to Genevra in a sacred vow, and the depth of emotion that throbbed through the words brought a blur of tears to Matthew's eyes. This is how it should always be, he thought, and when the clergyman turned to him and said, 'Who gives this woman...' Matthew handed Genevra into the keeping of the man she loved, knowing that God's will was surely being done this day.

Bright sunshine flooded through the glass doors which led out on to the balcony, brighter sunshine than Genevra had ever seen in England this early in the morning. But she and Luke had flown out of England after the wedding, and they were spending one glorious month alone in this beautiful villa on the French Riviera.

She stretched with lazy pleasure, then turned on her side to gaze possessively at her new husband. As much as she loved Johnny and Felicity, Genevra felt an almost overwhelming greed to have Luke to herself for a while. And it wouldn't hurt the children. Not when they had Auntie May and Grandpa indulging their every whim.

Luke was still asleep, but she couldn't resist touching him. The sensuality of last night's love-making was still a vivid memory, and she ran featherlight fingertips over his back, savouring the texture of firm flesh and muscle. He stirred and she pressed her mouth to his shoulder to prevent his turning over.

'Are you awake?' she whispered.

'No. This has to be a dream,' he answered, but she heard the smile in his voice.

'If you dare doubt that it's real, I'll scratch you all over,' she threatened, pressing her nails into the pit of his back.

He gave a lovely, deep chuckle, and started to roll towards her.

'No. Don't move,' she commanded, pushing him back and snuggling her body around his. 'I've got you covered and I want the truth.'

'I love you,' he said with very satisfactory fervour.

'I know that,' she said, feeling blissfully smug about it. 'What I don't know is what happened to your mole.'

He heaved himself up, dropping her back on to the pillows as he loomed over her. 'What mole?' he asked laughingly.

'The mole near the pit of your back, and don't tell me you don't know what mole,' she insisted with mock truculence. 'That mole has given me a bad time. That mole has a lot to answer for. If that mole had been where it should have been, you wouldn't have lasted as Christian Nemo past that first night at the Manoir.'

'Good God! Are you saying that you deliberately seduced me to look for a mole?'

'That was the plan. But things got carried away a bit. You always did have this terribly distracting influence on me, Luke.'

He shook his head at her, a bemused grin on his face. 'You really were certain it was me?'

'Well, then I was. Things got a little trickier later on. But I do think it's time you cleared up the mystery of the mole.'

She pouted in mock sulkiness and he kissed her, kissed her so thoroughly and erotically that Genevra forgot all about the mole. And the kissing didn't stop at her mouth.

'What are you doing?' she gasped, squirming with sensuous delight.

'Seducing you as deliberately as you seduced me.'

And he showed her no mercy at all, ravishing her senses with such a wicked knowledge of how to give pleasure that Genevra was still tingling with it long after the climax of their passion for each other was reached and passed.

'It was cut out,' he murmured, nibbling her ear teasingly.

'What was cut out?' Genevra mumbled, sighing with sweet contentment.

'During one of the operations. The surgeon mentioned it in passing. Thought he might as well take it off while he was wielding the knife.'

Laughter suddenly bubbled up in her, and she rolled on to her back to give full vent to it, her eyes twinkling exultantly at Luke until she caught her breath enough to speak. 'You mean, you didn't have that mole deliberately removed?'

His face was stamped with surprised innocence. 'Never thought of it.'

'Oh, Luke! Don't ever try to deceive me again. You're hopeless at it.'

He sighed and drew her back into his embrace, stroking her with almost reverent tenderness. 'You are everything to me, Genevra. You always will be. Don't ever doubt that, whatever I might do. But I promise you now, there will never be anything but truth between us.'

'And love,' she whispered.

'There was always love,' he said, hugging her tightly to him. 'Always.'

# Harlequin Presents

## Coming Next Month

Available in April wherever paperback books are sold, or through Harlequin Reader Service:

In the U.S.
901 Fuhrmann Blvd.
P.O. Box 1397
Buffalo, N.Y. 14240-1397

In Canada
P.O. Box 603
Fort Erie, Ontario
L2A 5X3

# Have You Ever Wondered If You Could Write A Harlequin Novel?

Here's great news—Harlequin is offering a series of cassette tapes to help you do just that. Written by Harlequin editors, these tapes give practical advice on how to make your characters—and your story—come alive. There's a tape for each contemporary romance series Harlequin publishes.

Mail order only

All sales final

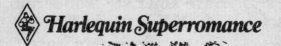

# Harlequin Superromance

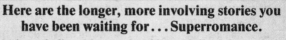

**Here are the longer, more involving stories you have been waiting for...Superromance.**

Modern, believable novels of love, full of the complex joys and heartaches of real people.

Intriguing conflicts based on today's constantly changing life-styles.

Four new titles every month.
Available wherever paperbacks are sold.